The Best Government Money Can Buy

Ernie Webb

ISBN: 0-9708102-3-7

DEDICATION

To Pat, my wife of 48 years,
who has supported me through
peace and war, good times and bad.

CONTENTS

Acknowledgments   i

1   No Guts, No Glory   1

2   The Competition   15

3   A Little Something Here, A Little Something There   27

4   Beijing, China   43

5   From Sea to Shining Sea: 55
    Activity Across America

6   The Business of Washington   60

7   Once More With Feeling   71

8   A Chink in the Armor   89

9   Colossus in Command   99

10   Somewhere Near the Arizona-Mexico Border   107

11   Somewhere in China   116

12   The FBI and Homeland Security   123

13   Home-Grown Jihadists   130

14   Happy on the Bayou   137

15   Springtime in Washington   147

16   Economics are Trump   158

17   Reap the Rewards of Corruption   169

18   When the Chickens Come Home to Roost   178

19   The Aftermath   182

20   Once More: Beijing   185

ACKNOWLEDGMENTS

Thanks to my editor, Carol von Raesfeld,
The von Raesfeld Agency, Henderson, NV

Thanks to my neighbor, Mike Cullen,
for his encouragement, editing input, and assistance
with finishing this book.

Thanks to Dorothy Hardy
for the outstanding cover design

Thanks to the men and women of our Armed Forces
who suffer hardships while protecting our country.

God bless America!

One

"No Guts, No Glory"

Whut! The bullet sped through the barrel and out into the night. The shooter felt the recoil, but remained focused on his target. The homeless man clutched at his chest as the round tore through his flesh. His legs gave way and he slid into an awkward sitting position against the wall, casting an eerie shadow from the dim streetlight. His still smoking cigarette fell to the wet sidewalk. His head twitched and then tilted forward. A dark stain seeped into his jacket, soaking his fingers in blood.

Whut! The silencer muffled the sound of the second shot. The man's body jerked awkwardly and then he fell onto his side in a lifeless heap—fresh debris on a city street.

No guts, huh? Matthew thought about Bezzos' cheap shot during the debate, then picking up his spent brass, he left the scene. He hadn't felt this good in a long time.

Early the following morning the body was discovered and reported to the police, who conducted a limited and perfunctory investigation. Street deaths were fairly common. The District of Columbia police didn't have the time to fully investigate every occurrence. There were too many important things on which to concentrate so the department had to establish priorities. The police report did note that this "kill" was a bit unusual. Both rounds were from a high-powered rifle. Both rounds were hollow-point, designed for maximum damage. Both shots were well placed. Either shot could have been the cause of death. Together, there was no doubt about the outcome—this shooter had obviously had some training.

"Why the second round?" asked one detective.

"Good question," replied his partner. "Probably some stupid argument between these two guys – you know, stole his shopping cart or something and the shooter wanted to make sure he made the kill. People sometimes just do crazy things. Or, this is one extremely efficient psycho – he leaves little room for mistakes. Could be a pro."

"Except who would hire a pro to make a hit on some homeless guy?" asked his partner. "There's gotta be some rationale. No witnesses, no brass, no clues?"

"Nope. Area was clean."

"Anyone hear anything? See anything?"

"Don't know. No one is coming forward. But we did find this in the vic's wallet." The detective offered a picture of the dead man with some buddies. All were wearing U.S. Army uniforms bearing the shoulder patch of the 101st Airborne Division "Screaming Eagles." Each had weapons and the surrounding area looked like the standard pictures from Iraq or Afghanistan.

"Looks like the guy spent some time in the Army. From the looks of it, he shoulda stayed in. Three hots and a cot beats the hell outta living on the streets – or dying on them."

"Yeah. Damn, I hate this," the lead detective said. "It's such a waste. Here's a guy who fought for this country, probably saw some of his buddies die – then he comes home and now has nothing – no home, apparently no family – nothin'... and then to have to go out like this.

"What a shame...but ya know, lots of these guys coming back have a tough time readjusting. It's a mental thing. Tough to get back in the groove."

"Yeah, what do they call it? PTSD or somethin'? What's it mean? I forget."

"Post Traumatic Stress Disorder."

"Oh, yeah, thanks. Causes some of them to do crazy stuff, huh? Do you think it might have been another veteran – you know – a guy with that PTSD problem himself?"

"Could be, but I think that's a long shot. I think there's more to it than that."

Meanwhile, Matthew had returned to his apartment, cleaned his rifle, hidden everything behind a false door in his closet, taken a shower, and then gone to bed. He felt relaxed and fell asleep enjoying a great sense of pride and accomplishment. He slept well and when he awoke the next morning and thought about last night's event, his body tingled with excitement.

What a rush! Both shots right on target! Damn, I'm good! No doubt about it, he's dead. I coulda made it in combat. I'll show you guts! He clicked on the TV for information on his exploits.

"In other news," the announcer reported, "a homeless man was found shot to death in Anacostia early this morning. No further information is available. The police are trying to locate any family members. If you have any information concerning this man or this crime, please notify the police at the number shown on the bottom of the screen. And now the weather..."

"Yeeaah!" Matthew Tibideaux shouted, pumping his fist in the air. "I coulda been a goddamn sniper! Too bad Bezzos wasn't there!" Tibideaux's self-esteem had been restored. The emotion was indescribable; he felt like a giant turbo transformer robot, the kind his kids used to play with around the house. Or did he feel more like Spiderman – his own childhood hero? Whatever, it felt great! He knew that once again "I'm the man!"

"Yeeaaaah!" He danced around the apartment, feeling his testosterone level surging! The phone rang. He picked it up after the first ring. "Tibideaux here."

"Senator," his aide wasted no time. "Just wanted to know if you had any last minute changes to your presentation to the Senate Finance Committee today."

"No," Matthew replied. "Everything looks good. I'll see you in about an hour."

"Okay, Senator, thanks. We'll have everything ready."

* * *

Matthew Tibideaux, the junior Senator from Louisiana, had been in Washington slightly more than four years. He'd won his seat by surviving a vicious campaign where he'd played heavily in two primary areas: One, the need for more jobs in Louisiana, a state still hovering near 10% unemployment; and Two, the patriotism factor. An avid hunter, he was also endorsed by the NRA. Having been a member of the U.S. Army Reserve, he capitalized on his military service, frequently emphasizing that his opponent, John Bezzos, a successful businessman, had never served in the military. Since coming to Washington, Tibideaux had developed a penchant for citing his military service as a means of adding gravitas to his pronouncements on national security.

"Those of us who have been in war understand the value of freedom," he'd begin. He'd soften his voice and then he'd slowly nod his head. The crowd would nod with him. He'd look out at the crowd and then pause. Those in the crowd would collectively catch their breath. His words would pierce their souls. His eyes would hold them fast and they would feel a great sense of awe at his undaunted courage under fire. Then having totally captivated them, he would resume. He was extremely effective and could almost feel himself capture the hearts and minds of his constituents.

Johnny Bezzos had not taken the loss lightly. He had pressed on with investigations into Tibideaux's military service, intending to challenge his re-election bid. Bezzos had issued a number of disparaging comments about Tibideaux's service and was pushing hard to discredit the Senator before the next senatorial election campaign – the claim of combat service was his trump card. Bezzos knew the claims were false. One of the men who worked for Bezzos had been in Tibideaux's outfit in the Iraq War. Although the man was reluctant to say anything negative about Tibideaux, he'd made a few comments that inspired Bezzos to continue the investigation. The month prior, Bezzos had conducted a press conference in New Orleans where he'd responded to an earlier speech by Tibideaux.

"Yesterday," Bezzos began, "Matthew Tibideaux, the junior senator from Louisiana, once again lied to the people of Louisiana and America. He told us that he was a combat veteran. I believe his exact words were 'Those of us who have been in war understand the importance of freedom.' Well, truth is – he has *never* been to war! First, he only served six months when his unit stayed an entire year. Second, when his unit went into Iraq, he somehow managed to stay in Kuwait, a *non*-combat area, where the loudest thing he heard was the backfire of a Kuwaiti taxi! His buddies went to war and many of them suffered the ultimate consequences – but Tibideaux? Don't let him pull the wool over your eyes. He stayed in a safe zone...and then he came home early to be a politician! He's no hero!"

With the applause of his supporters, John Bezzos unofficially kicked off his campaign to unseat the junior senator from Louisiana. Then turning away and unaware that the microphone was still on, Bezzos muttered to an aide, "He's a coward without the guts to pull the trigger on anything tougher than a bunny rabbit. He couldn't make it in combat."

Elements of the press and members of Senator Tibideaux's party denounced Bezzos and demanded an immediate apology. They called his statements "un-American, barbaric, and an affront to civility." The liberal press was outraged. "Is there no longer any civility in America? Do we no longer respect our members of Congress?" they asked. They began an immediate search deep into Bezzos' past in an attempt to "find any possible dirt." What they found was what they already knew: he was ethically clean, but blunt, even crude in his speech. One liberal cable newscaster called him a "foul-mouthed, undisciplined muckraker." Affecting an attitude of feigned outrage and pretending to speak from a position of superior intelligence, yet another said, "He is merely another of those white-haired old people who belong to that radical Tea Party movement that has damaged our nation's political processes." The commentator added, "Bezzos was never even in the military. How can he judge?"

In response to the faux outrage, Bezzos replied, "Unlike the senator, I have not created a false Hollywood persona. If you must hide behind a façade, you are a coward. If my words, which are the truth, offend you – get a life! If he'll lie about this, what else will he lie about? Too many politicians have lied to the American people for far too long on far too many issues. Louisiana deserves better – in fact, America deserves better.

As to my having never been in the military, yes, that is true and I'm not ashamed to admit it. I respect those who have served, but there are other ways to serve. I have served the people of my state in different ways and I am proud of my record. And as to the liberal media, I hear more intelligent sounds coming from the splat of cow droppings on my daddy's farm than I do from your opinions on just about any subject; plus the cow dung has a sweeter, cleaner smell. You are merely purveyors of nonsensical and totally biased blather."

A few liberal broadcasters understood the meaning of his words. They were offended, but didn't know how to respond.

Tibideaux was advised by multiple colleagues to ignore the attacks. "You cannot let this thing drag you down," they told him. "Stay above the mud-slinging, but you also need to stop talking about your military service. Don't give him any more ammunition. Who do you know in the press who'd be willing to carry this fight for you? That way, you stay clean, but Bezzos gets slapped around."

"I don't know," Tibideaux replied. "I just want to beat the shit out of him."

"Can't do that," his aides replied. "You have to do this the Washington way."

But Matthew wanted desperately to fight back, even though what Bezzos had said about his war record was true. The situation worsened as several of the newspapers and late night comedians considered the story to be worthwhile, newsworthy—and funny. Cartoons depicted him with a toy rifle, frightened and running from a stuffed rabbit that squealed gleefully as it chased him across the page. Comedians ridiculed him. Tibideaux was furious that his courage and manhood had been called into question. It was embarrassing. He didn't like this feeling of embarrassment and the rage boiled up inside of him, making him feel ill each time he thought about it. Once he was so sick that he vomited his lunch into the toilet which left a foul taste in his mouth. *Phewt! Phewt*! He tried desperately to spit it out.

"I am not a coward," he shouted to himself over and over. "I do too have the guts to pull the trigger and by God, I will prove it! I'll make them stop laughing at me."

Silently, he cursed himself for not having gone on at least one combat mission and he was jealous of those who had. "By God, I'll show them," he shouted as he punched the walls of his apartment. He quietly avoided most of his committee meetings that week, advising his aides that he was working on some draft proposals and needed some "alone" time. He imagined some of the politicians on the other side would be whispering about him in the halls of Congress and he just couldn't stand to face any such situation. Back in his apartment he calculated and considered many forms of revenge.

How did this situation develop? he wondered. He'd always considered himself to be fearless. The people who knew him, or knew *of* him, believed him to be fearless. In high school he'd played both baseball and football. In football he was known as a vicious linebacker who seemed to enjoy contact – the more the better. "Heyaah!" he'd yell on especially vicious tackles and then he'd stand over the downed runner and taunt him. He was known throughout the conference for his hard-hitting style.

In baseball, he'd led the league in stolen bases. He recalled the many times he'd sprinted off first base, headed for second base like a runaway train. He remembered the great adrenaline rush as he vaulted towards second base, just as the catcher released the ball and then he'd throw his body with wild abandon towards the base. *I kept that one foot low to hook the bag and the other one HIGH – with CLEATS UP!! I cut a bunch of them!*

Matthew gritted his teeth and grinned as he recalled many a second basemen who had let a catcher's throw get past him because he was focused more on avoiding those cleats than on catching the ball. And as every athlete knows, you can't make the play if you don't have the ball. *I scared the shit out of 'em!* Matthew had ignored the many bruises such play produced on his own body, as well as the bloody gash that left a nasty scar on his upper lip. *I was fearless and they all knew it!*

One weekend during Mardi Gras, Matthew and some friends were driving home from a party in a neighboring town when their car was hit by a runaway truck. Thrown from the vehicle, they all received a few minor cuts and bruises, except one—a close friend who died in the collision.

Matthew had tried to revive him. He gave him CPR. He slapped the boy's arms and legs to spur circulation. He shook him and made jokes about not giving up. "C'mon, this is no time to be acting crazy," he yelled. "Get up! I ain't gonna carry your ass home. This is no time to joke around! Get up!"

It was all to no avail. Matthew held his friend and watched as the boy's eyes glazed over and then rolled back into his head as his life slipped away. Matthew felt his friend's life energy depart and the body grew cold. In the early morning chill his friend's blood that covered Matthew's hands and arms also grew cold. Matthew stared in disbelief. He couldn't shake the realization that his friend was dead. He was gone! It was over. It was so final!

In the course of the following weeks, Matthew tried to understand, but nothing made any sense. Cuts and bruises were things from which you could recover – no big deal. They were part of life – life lived to the fullest. But death? It's all over – it really is final! There's no healing, no matter how badly you want to have the nightmare end. No jokes about the hit you took – or made on someone else to deserve a particular hurt. It's over! Unable to control his emotions, Matthew cried through the funeral, nearly losing it as his friend's casket was lowered into the ground. He never forgot. Matthew still played sports with abandon, but always in the back of his mind there was one thought: *Don't ever do anything that could risk life and death.* Even now he could still hear the sound of the dirt hitting the casket.

Years later when his unit was shipped to Kuwait, en route to Iraq, Matthew used all of his political skills to remain in Kuwait – in charge of resupply – rather than risk going into Iraq. They were killing people in Iraq! Americans were dying. He didn't fear going into battle and getting wounded, but he would not risk that finality of death. He would not go into combat. He could not face the finality! He'd already had all the death he could stand. Occasionally, he'd awaken from a dream in which he saw his own body with the listless eyes and the limp body, just like his friend's. Deep down inside he promised himself that he wouldn't face death in Iraq. He'd been able to rationalize his decision. After all – resupply is important and he was the smartest young officer in the unit. However, his friends didn't share his rationalization and Matthew could sense the difference in their attitude towards him. They no longer respected him. He knew it and resented it.

His wife, Nicole, tried to console him when he arrived home for the weekend, but to no avail.

"Honey," she pleaded, "please, let it go. The people of Louisiana love you. They won't tolerate him attacking you. Look at the jobs you've brought to the state and the efforts you're making to solve so many problems. You're a fighter and Louisiana needs fighters in these tough times. I love you and can't bear seeing you like this."

"But don't you see?" Matthew argued. "He's challenged my honor and my courage! No one has ever challenged my honor... no one!" He was lying to himself and to her, and he knew it. True, no one had openly challenged him, but some challenges are hidden and known only between the challenged and the challengers. Waves of memories swept over him—the looks of his fellow soldiers as they boarded the trucks for the combat zone while he stayed behind never left his mind. He could still recall the looks of scorn on their faces. Upon his return to the U.S. and when he ran for public office, he couldn't call upon any of his fellow soldiers to help him – or to speak up for him. Their absence and their silence were obvious. In their own way, they were still challenging him.

"Look," one of them offered in a private conversation. "He wimped out on us when it came time to stand up, so I, for one, will not support him; however, he did wear the uniform, so I will not attack him either. Once upon a time, he was one of us. I think our silence is the best approach."

The others agreed and none gave support to his political efforts. At the same time, none of them openly supported his opponent.

But I'm a U.S. Senator! I've brought jobs to Louisiana. I'm a good civil servant! What else do I have to do? Why won't they support me? I did a good job on the resupply missions. I did my part. He tried desperately to rationalize his decision, but deep down he knew. He couldn't shake this terrible feeling of inadequacy. He knew he had to do something. He owed it to himself.

He spent the weekend cleaning and caring for his favorite rifle, a Remington Woodsmaster 30.06, model 742, semi-automatic. He always felt better when he caressed its smooth stock. It had a power of its own and when he held it, he shared in that power. It had been given to him as a gift years ago when he was a kid. He hunted with it often until he went away to college. It had remained in his room for many years and it had never been registered. He hadn't used it since his return from Kuwait because he'd been too busy campaigning for office. He loved the feel of it and as he held it, turned it in his hands, he felt a warmth and sense of peace flow over him. He began to service it – the way his father had taught him. As he oiled and caressed the gun, his self-confidence returned. *I know how to use this. I'll show them,* he promised himself. *No one will ever laugh at me again.*

He decided to drive back to Washington rather than fly, so that he could carry his Remington with him. He drove with a light-heartedness that he hadn't known for some time. Once back in Washington, he made several trips to nearby firing ranges to calibrate his marksmanship. As a boy, he had been quite accurate, but now he possessed a drive to be not only good, but to be an expert in his use of this weapon. It didn't take long for him to regain his touch. He loved the feel of his rifle and he enjoyed the recoil against his shoulder. Soon it was all bulls-eyes! "Awright!" he would shout as the rounds tore through the paper targets. "Awright!" *I really could have been a sniper.* But there's only a fleeting, shallow satisfaction to be derived from shooting paper targets. *A man... a true man should have greater targets. On my mother's grave, I swear I will have those targets.*

His shooting of the homeless person had been completely random. He hadn't gone out searching for some homeless person, it was all merely coincidence. He'd just had an overwhelming urge to shoot something – a worthy target – anything to prove to himself that he could pull the trigger on something bigger than a rabbit! And there he was – a target. Later, as he reviewed his actions, he began to rationalize.

I did a good thing – a service to the city. These bums are just a drain on society. I probably saved the city thousands of dollars by getting him off the streets. Just another instance of doing my civic duty. I do a lot of good. Why can't I get any respect?

Immediately he felt the same wave of excitement and power as he had at the moment when he'd pulled the trigger and killed that man. He grinned and pranced around his apartment when suddenly a voice spoke to him. It stopped him in his tracks. It was a voice he'd never heard before—a powerful voice and it came from within his own head. He didn't recognize it.

Matthew.

Matthew wanted to answer, but he was too confused. Where was this voice coming from? He didn't recognize the voice, so he waited.

Matthew, I am Colossus, the Turbo Avenger. I right wrongs and punish the guilty! I am with you, even when no one else is! I know that you have courage. Together we will right wrongs and punish the guilty!

Tibideaux was still confused, but he liked what he heard. "Who are you?" he asked.

I am Colossus. I am your friend. I am your inner courage. I am you. The completed you! Together, we are strong. Together, we will gain you new respect.

"I don't know you!" Tibideaux shouted.

I am the inner you.

"What? Am I goin' fuckin' crazy? Are you like an alter-ego thing?

Laughing, the voice replied. *No, you're not crazy. I am part of you. I am part of your inner strength. I am here to help you gain the respect you deserve. Together we will right wrongs and punish the guilty! I have been with you all along, but I have been quiet. I was there every time you made a fearless slide into second base, but I was silent. You did not need me then. The time has come when you need me and now I am here.*

Yes, Tibideaux thought. *My inner strength. I will right wrongs and punish the guilty!* He marched around the room, moving his arms and legs in the jerky motions of a robot, occasionally pretending to take aim on some imaginary enemy—and pulling the trigger. Each time the imaginary enemy crumpled up in pain and then died. This feeling of power was incredible! It was warm and tingly, and he didn't have to share it with anyone! It was all his! When initiated by his own actions, death didn't seem so terrible, so final. It was merely the logical outcome of his superior skills. Matthew had become a master at the art of rationalization. During his four plus years in government, he had learned his lessons well. It also made the Bezzos event seem trivial. *He's a punk. I beat his ass in the election and I can beat him again. I am the man!*

Once again Tibideaux became a force on the political scene. Everyone admired his courage and his ability to fight for his constituents. Each day he would stride down the hallways and into the offices of Congress. He was an example for others to see and to follow.

His wife and children missed him during the week, but they were proud of the work he was doing. They agreed to do as much together on the weekends as possible; however, family times were often limited since Matthew had to attend so many political functions, even when he returned to Louisiana. There was always another fundraiser or charity event where he needed to be seen. The family understood and waited for the few moments he could be with them and they could have his undivided attention.

Two

"The Competition"

New Orleans, Louisiana

"That was a real smart move, Johnny," Bezzos' campaign manager laughed. "Leaving the mike on when you talked about the rabbit!"

"Hey, that was not intentional," Bezzos replied, holding his big hands up. "I think he's a liar and a coward, but I won't do crap like that on purpose. I really thought the mic was off. I've even thought about apologizing, but that would be playing the same old political game as most of these other politicians – you know, make a statement that's harmful, then back off and apologize so the voters think you're a nice guy. You do the damage to your opponent and then calm the anger against yourself. That's bullshit – no honesty there. I believe what I said – just should have said it up front... and I do need to be careful. In the future, I don't want anything to come across as sneaky. Remember, he has a wife and kids. I don't want to embarrass them. We have a strong enough case on him to play it up front and in the open, okay?"

The staff all nodded agreement.

"And I want you guys to help me. If I slip up on something, speak up – right then! Help me to not fall into that old trap – you know, 'open mouth, insert foot.'" The group laughed.

"I know, it's my responsibility first – I'm just asking you to help, okay? Oh, one more thing," he added. "Tibideaux is fair game – but no lies. And if any of you try to embarrass his wife and kids, you're out – but not 'til I cut your nuts off and nail 'em over the courthouse door. Any questions?" The staff laughed and understood.

"Well," one young staffer spoke up, "I do have a question. A friend of mine has a cousin who is a Congressional staffer. He says that it's understood that once you get elected, stuff starts to come your way, and it's tough to turn away. What about that? I mean, if someone comes to us with something under the table – do you want to hear about it? What do you want us to do?"

"What kinda 'stuff' are you referring to?" Johnny asked.

"You know – stuff."

"No, I don't know, but it sounds to me that you're talking about something crooked – graft, fraud, corruption – is that right?"

"Yeah, do we go along or what?"

Johnny's jaw stiffened. "Actually, that's a great question... and here's the answer. "Our country was once the paradigm of the world. Now, a good number of our politicians are a joke. They can even be censured by other members of Congress – and instead of getting the boot they become the keynote speaker at the next convention. That's wrong. When our elected officials are corrupt, it sets a horrible example for the rest of the country, like – you know – 'It's okay to take a bribe... after all, members of Congress do it all the time.' I do not subscribe to this philosophy. I guess this opinion of politicians started with Harry Truman. You know, U.S. President number 33, when he jokingly said, 'My choice early in life was either to be a piano player in a whorehouse or a politician. And to tell the truth, there's hardly any difference.' Actually, I don't think he was joking; but I don't intend to be either. If I am going to run for office – and hopefully achieve it, me and my staff, we will adhere to the ideals that this nation is truly the 'city on the hill' and we will be true to America's values. Is that perfectly clear?"

There was a nodding of heads and no more questions.

* * *

"Kinda got a bit in front of yourself, didn't you?" Melinda Bezzos asked her husband that evening as they sat down for dinner.

"Yeah," Johnny replied. "It's tougher than I thought. And I never was good at keeping my mouth shut. That's why I knew I could never hold a job in some big corporate outfit. Knew I'd piss somebody off along the way."

"Now, there's an understatement," Melinda laughed. "But, Honey, your frank and honest approach has helped in the business, hasn't it? I mean people know that with you what they see is what they get – and you won't cheat anybody. People know that. That's gotta be worth something. It sure is with me. 'Course, sometimes you're a bit crude," she smiled and cocked her head to the side.

"You know," he chuckled, "you really have a knack for saying just the right thing! Think you could teach me a bit of that – knowing when to say the right thing?"

"I'd love to," she replied.

"Thanks, I think so... the honesty, I mean," he said, referring to her earlier comment. "But I'm not sure that counts for much anymore, which is why I got into this rat race in the first place. And as to the crude bit, I get so damn tired of hearing these politicians beat around the bush and never saying anything clear enough for folks to understand. I may be crude, but when I'm finished, folks for sure know how I feel about a subject and what I would do to fix a problem. I grew up on a farm and on the farm you must face life as it is. You can't rationalize a crop to grow or a cow to give milk. If you don't plant at the right time, then water and cultivate properly you get no crops... and the cow can't and won't milk herself. That's real life and our politicians and the liberal press don't understand that. It's like they're all in some dream world of unreality. Unfortunately, fewer and fewer of our citizens understand that. Too many just want a handout.

You know, Honey, America seems to have lost the vision – the desire to reach out and make things happen. We seem to be more and more content with just waiting for the next handout. That gives the politicians a free rein to do all kinds of crap. I still believe that the best approach is not to give a 'hand out' but to offer a 'hand-up.' I thought when the Tea Party folks got voted in that we'd see a change, but now I'm not sure if they can change the system before the system changes them. You know, I bet even Tibideaux was a good guy at first. But then like my daddy used to say, 'If you wrestle with pigs, you're gonna smell like a pig.' It takes one helluva man – or woman – to resist the pig sties of Washington, but I guess it's been this way for a long time. Even back in the 1930s, Will Rogers said, 'Ain't it funny how many hundreds of thousands of soldiers we can recruit with nerve, but we just can't find one politician in a million with backbone.' I think that's where we are today."

Johnny's mind wandered back in time. He was seven – or maybe eight years old when his father decided it was time for him to start working on the farm. His father woke him and told him to go bring in the cows – while it was still dark! The family had a small herd of thirty-five milk cows and had not yet been able to buy automated milking machines, so the family still milked by hand. Johnny smiled as he remembered how proud he had been bringing the cows in – all of them, and quickly!   Standing there, admiring his work, his father approached him and said, "Well?"

"Well what, Dad?"

"Well, when are you going to finish the job?"

"But, they're all here," Johnny had insisted. "I got every one of them."

"Then you should have your bucket and be milking," his father had replied. "If you have a job to do, then do it right and all the way."

His father then called out three cows by name: Bessie, Three Spot, and Big Eyes. "Before you go to school each day, you bring all the cows in and then you milk those three."

Johnny didn't think it unusual that at the age of eight, he had a regular job before school. That was farm life, plain and simple. That was America when it was on top of the world.

"I know," his wife continued, unaware of his lapse into past memories. "Somebody needs to step up and fight all this stuff that's happening to our country. If folks like us don't get involved, we're gonna be in big trouble."

"Yeah, that's what you and me keep saying – sure hope something good comes out of all this. But for tonight, let's not talk about it anymore, okay?" Before she could answer, Johnny grabbed her. "Now give me a big kiss."

Melinda loved the feel of his arms around her. "You know," she said, softly stroking his thick, wavy brown hair, she returned his kiss. "I still feel like this is the safest place in the entire world, right here in your arms. It makes me feel all warm inside."

"And I love having you here, even more than I did the day we first said our vows. In fact, I love it more and more, every day." Gently he began rubbing her back.

"Careful now," she teased. "Don't start something you can't finish." They both laughed the soft, warm laugh of soul mates – like the cooing of two doves caressing each other in the warmth of an early sunrise on a young spring morning – committed to each other for life. They held each other close for several minutes, kissed, and then took a walk around the neighborhood.

"Do you remember our first dance?" Melinda asked.

"Yeah. What was that, eighth grade?"

"Yes. You were a big old clumsy farm boy. I still think you asked me to dance on a dare from that friend of yours. I knew better than to say yes because you were just a farm boy. In fact, I was sure you had cow dung on those boots! All the girls used to laugh about it!"

"Then why did you accept?"

"Dunno, I guess 'the devil made me do it,'" she laughed softly.

"Yeah, it was a dare... and I didn't expect you to say yes. I think I stepped on every one of your toes."

"You sure did. But even when you were clumsy, you were gentle. Weird." Again she laughed her soft laugh.

"Then, in high school, I thought I was gonna lose you because I couldn't play sports," he added. "I thought all the girls wanted to date only the sports guys – you know, the jocks."

"Well, that woulda been nice, but, you didn't have time. You had to help on the farm, especially after your mom died. Your dad needed you."

"Yeah, he took it hard... her dyin' and all. I guess we all did. The farm was a lot of work. I still would have liked to play some kinda sport, but what the hell. I still got you – and that was the best of all."

Johnny and Melinda had been high school sweethearts and had remained so, even when he went off to college. Johnny had held several odd jobs to pay for his tuition and room and board, but, after two years he could no longer afford the expense of college, so dropped out to work in the construction industry while still helping out on the family farm.   Good with his hands and a hard worker, he eventually built his own company as a building contractor. It had been a rough beginning. He had to be his own salesman as well as his own workforce. He spent many twelve-hour days in hard labor before he could afford to hire an assistant. Gradually, however, the business had grown and he had hired more and more workers. He demanded good work, but he treated them fairly.

He was known in the trade as an upfront guy with a penchant for crude – even foul language and colorful sayings. One in particular that his workers joked about was his quote "that's how the cow eats the cabbage!" when he wanted to make a point — like when someone would try to use some shortcut which diminished the quality of the work, Johnny would fire them on the spot. When the ex-employee tried to complain – or explain, Johnny would shake his head, and say, "Well, that's how the cow eats the cabbage. You purposely do a shabby job you don't get to keep the job. So get over it." Then he would turn to everyone else. "You screw up trying to do right and I will cover you all the way 'cause we all make mistakes – but when you purposely do something wrong, I can't afford to keep you around."

Everyone knew that cows and cabbages was the last word and there was no sense trying to argue with him. The decision had been made and to Johnny it was the only decision that could be made. "Cows and cabbages" was as right as anything could be.

He wasn't adverse to using his big hands in a fight. He had a tendency to argue – or debate – an issue just so far, then in frustration he would announce, "time for talkin' is over." Those folks around him all knew that statement would be followed by a huge roundhouse punch so most folks had learned to not push the conversation that far. To his credit, he had not been in a fight for several years, but his reputation still lingered.

Melinda's family had wanted her to go to college, but she knew they couldn't afford it. Seemed no matter how hard they worked, they just couldn't get ahead. Melinda had worked since she was fifteen, buying her own clothes to help the family.

"Mom, Dad, I've got something to tell you," she began one evening at dinner. "I've got a job as a receptionist downtown. Pay's not bad and it'll be steady. In a coupla years, I can earn enough for college."

"But Honey, we always had hopes you could be the first in our family to get a degree and not have to work like a peon for someone else." The disappointment in her father's eyes was heartbreaking.

"I know, Dad. I'll go, just not now. Maybe I can take a few courses at the community college, but I promise you – I will get a college degree."

"I know, Honey, but we so wanted you to go." In his heart, he knew she was right. They couldn't afford to help her.

"Hey! It'll wait. That college isn't going away. I'll still get my degree, you just wait and see."

"When that time comes, Melinda," her mother added, "we'll be here to help anyway we can."

"I know, Mom. You always have. I love you."

She later found work with a small engineering firm in Baton Rouge and she and Johnny were married a year later. She continued working with the engineering firm and keeping Johnny's business books at night until his business grew to where she could devote herself fulltime to their company and to their son. They employed approximately forty workers, and provided contract work for several smaller contractors, thus providing even more jobs. They made a great team. He ran the field work and she took care of all the administrative matters and accounting. Along the way, she continued to take evening courses, building up her credits until she had only one semester left.

"Time to hire you an assistant so you can take this semester off and finish your degree," said Johnny.

"But we can't do that. Too much work to do right here."

"Honey, we can make it happen. You made your folks a promise and we keep our promises."

"That's my daughter!" Her parents shouted when she walked onstage to receive her diploma. She waved to them, her face beaming with pride and happiness. She was proud of her diploma, but even more proud that she had kept her promise to her parents.

She and only she could push Johnny past the point of "time for talkin' is over" and keep him on track. He loved her far too much to ever lift a hand against her. He also knew that she'd probably respond with a big iron skillet or a baseball bat – something bigger and harder than his fist!

He loved her for so many reasons and her toughness was definitely one of them. One minute she could be driving a tractor for spring plowing and the next she'd be holding a child with the gentleness of an angel, while kissing away the pain of their latest "boo-boo." She was easygoing, yet no pushover. She could hold her own in almost any situation.

"She's sumpin' else," the workers were apt to remark.

"Yeah, paychecks always on time – and always right. She's damn smart."

"That's right... and if she hears you had a bit of a family set back, you probably gonna find a bit of extra cash in your pay envelope. Then she smiles and says, 'Tell your wife things will get better.' She's helped a bunch of us and I'm one of 'em."

"I hear tell she comes from workin' family stock," another worker replied, sending a spittle of tobacco juice onto the ground." She knows what it's like to fall on hard times – and she ain't never forgot it."

"Yeah, she's sumpin' alright," another chuckled. "And I damn sure wouldn't want to cross her. I bet she could be as mean as Johnny if she had a reason."

"Probably. She sure keeps him in line." They all grinned.

Richard Bezzos graduated from LSU and then joined the company as lead salesman and estimator. Built like his dad and full of energy, Richard still worked at least one day per week with the laborers so he could remain fully aware of what the workers faced every day.

Powerfully built and knowledgeable in the trade, Richard was welcomed by the workers since he didn't shirk from the tough work – and he had real calluses on his hands from the labor – not the smooth, well-manicured hands of the wealthy kids who got jobs because their daddy pulled some strings. Plus he had a great sense of humor and made them laugh – a much needed commodity in the day of such high unemployment and inflation. He'd been a good, but not spectacular athlete in high school and didn't participate in college. Instead, he fell in love with music – a mix of Country and Cajun.

Occasionally, after one of those days working with his daddy's crews, he would unload a cooler of beer from his truck, break out his guitar, and call to the other workers. "Hey, time to unwind a bit, 'less you got some immediate plans!" He would sit on the tailgate of his pickup and start playing Cajun tunes.

The crews would gather 'round, yelling out the names of their favorite tunes while filling plastic cups with cold beer. He never held them more than about thirty minutes because he didn't want them leaving drunk or being gone too long from their families. He just wanted to help them relax a bit after a hard day. The workers all had their own favorite songs and would sing along when he played their favorite.

Largely because of his dad's reputation, he'd never been in a fight his entire life; however, everyone suspected that if need be – he could and would fight and it wouldn't be pretty for his opponent.

Richard was also one of those fiercely family loyal kids, who adored his grandfather. Once or twice a month, he'd spend the entire weekend at his grandfather's farm. They no longer milked the cows by hand, but Richard knew how to hook up the machines and considered it his job to "get the milking done" on those visits. He loved those visits, as did Granddad. Walking side by side in the "milking barn," his grandfather would occasionally reach over and pretend to inspect the machine hookups Richard had made.

"What're you doin', Granddad?" Richard would ask.

"Well, you bein' a 'city-boy' and all, I jest thought I best check your work. City boys ain't used to real work, ya know!"

"Well, mebbe som'day I'll larn," Richard would tease back, mimicking a Southern drawl. They'd both smile, knowing the warmth of this deep family connection. Love is a wonderful thing; tender love is even greater, but when it comes wrapped in a sense of humor, it exceeds all bounds.

Granddad also enjoyed a bit of "toe-tappin'" to a good Cajun beat and played a pretty mean fiddle 'his own self'! In the evening, they'd sit on the front porch of the old farmhouse and play. It was not unusual for several of the neighbors to stop by and join in the festivities. No one came empty-handed. Down on a farm, everyone shares in everything. When one works, all work. When one plays, all play. The American farm may be the greatest institution ever known to man. There's always lots to eat and drink, good old "down home" fun...and, of course, hard work.

Johnny was tickled at the closeness of his son and father; and of the ease with which Richard moved around the farm. "This is all good preparation for life, son," he'd say. "Even being in the barn with all that cow shit should be a lesson in life. Once you learn what it smells like, you never forget it. As you get older, lots of folks will try to win you over with their own brand of cow shit, but once you know how it smells, you can detect it and protect yourself. Your granddad used to tell me, 'Life is kinda like spending time crossing through a cow pasture. You decide which way you want to go—stay on course—and try not to step in anything—like cowshit.'" Johnny had never forgotten the smell or this advice, and neither had his son.

On occasion, the two of them would get into a heavy discussion of politics and philosophy. Each time, Johnny would remind Richard, "Don't get sucked in by those folks spreadin' their version of cowshit to make the world look like its run their way."

"I know, Dad," Richard would reply. "But sometimes it's hard to tell... and folks are different now. Most folks don't care about the country or take any responsibility for what they think or do as long as they get their way."

"Yeah, I think we're headed for big trouble. Once we get over one-half the folks with the notion that they can get everything they want from handouts and no responsibility of their own, we're on a downhill slide. Beggars just waitin' for China or somebody to kick our ass... and we're damn near there."

Often, they'd go on for hours and when they did it was Melinda who'd be the one to bring them back into the real world.

"When you two 'cow shit philosophers' get a minute, I could use a hand in here!"

They knew immediately it was time to go help — and to stop talking politics.

Three

"A Little Something Here, A Little Something There"

A short time later, a reinvigorated Senator Tibideaux adjusted his tie and then walked confidently into the office of the Senate Majority Leader. Tibideaux was a bright, fast-rising star in his party. He had made all the right moves, voted as directed, and with his handsomely rugged good looks he was a public relations asset for almost any bill or program the party wanted to push, that is until the recent Bezzos attacks.

"You wanted to see me?" he asked.

"Yes, come in." The Majority Leader pointed to a chair opposite his desk and continued his telephone conversation. The Louisiana senator took a seat and waited. He was tempted to try and look under the Majority Leader's desk, but decided against it. There were rumors about the Leader he wanted to confirm.

Finally, the Leader finished and hung up the phone. "Well," he asked. "How are you?"

"Fine, Senator. What's the purpose of this meeting?" Tibideaux again strained slightly to see behind the Majority Leader's desk without being too obvious. It was well known on the hill that the Majority Leader had a fetish. It was rumored that he considered himself to be like Bill Clinton. To satisfy this fetish he frequently brought young female interns into his office where he required them to position themselves in the hollow of his massive desk and perform a "Monica" act on him. He reportedly carved a "notch" in an inner desk drawer to mark each occasion. His constituents back home were all familiar with the rumor but continued to vote for him because he was adept at "bringing home the pork." His constituents didn't care about his morals or his ethics as long as he brought money back to the state – and the Majority Leader was well aware of their attitude.

The Majority Leader laughed slightly and leaned back in his chair. He'd loosened his tie from around his massive neck, which made him look even more like a bulldog than normal. He swung his massive shoulders around to squarely face Tibideaux. His bushy eyebrows were raised slightly in a sign of amusement. Tibideaux had seen that look before. The Majority Leader was a master at the use of power and he knew how to get legislation passed. The raised eyebrows were usually the prelude to a "put-up or shut-up" conversation. Tibideaux knew that whatever the meeting was to be about, any negotiation would not last long. It was the way things were done "on the Hill." You scratch my back and I scratch yours. Your constituents expected you to produce for your district or state: that's why they sent you to Washington. A little pork here, a little pork there made everyone happy. In the grand scheme of things it was no big deal. And if you were able to pick up a little something for yourself along the way, so much the better. After all, everyone was getting something. *It is the great American way,* Tibideaux thought, grinning at his own joke.

"I understand that you're wavering on the new transportation appropriations bill and I believe it's time to commit. Now the President wants this bill as part of his domestic program. I want this bill because I have earmarked a few items for my state." Tibideaux understood that if the Majority Leader had some "earmarked" money in this bill, then it was a personal issue. Even though many members of both the House and the Senate had campaigned against earmarks, there was always some way around it. Most Congressmen and women recognized that all of the noise made about "earmarks" was only for public consumption. Once the doors were closed, politicians took care of themselves. "And," he continued, "I want you to want this bill. We are only two votes short. So, what will it take to get you on board? What do you want for your state? Everything is on the table. The negotiations are on, but not for long. I need to expedite the resolution of this issue.

"Understand?" Tibideaux nodded. "And let me make it clear that what goes around comes around."

Tibideaux understood the implication. *This is a great opportunity to get myself in the good graces of the Leader and maybe get something more out of it as well.*

So, what do you want in return?" the Leader asked. "Besides getting Bezzos off your ass?"

Tibideaux was pleased, but was careful not to show it. He ignored the Bezzos comment. He'd been trying to determine how he could best get the support he needed for his client – Mr. Yao of Yao Enterprises. And, of course, that would also help the voters in his state. The Majority Leader had made this almost too easy. All he had to do was to sell his vote to the Majority Leader. That was easy enough to do since he really didn't care about the transportation bill one way or the other. He also knew that since the Majority Leader had initiated this little bartering session, he'd be true to his word. He was a master at this game of give-and-take. He was also the master of "breaking your legs" politically, if you crossed him. Tibideaux sensed that this bill was important enough to the Majority Leader that his vote was worth more to the Leader than just money. The *quid pro quo* here would not be a direct exchange of money – it would be more subtle than that.

"Okay," Tibideaux responded. "I need that bill to include an addendum for a substantial increase for the communications portion of NASA, especially in the State of Louisiana."

"That's it?" The Majority Leader was puzzled.

"Well, I also want some say in which companies get the contracts on this new communications software," Tibideaux replied.

"So, if I okay what you want, we get your vote. Agreed?"

"Agreed." Tibideaux rose, shook the Majority Leader's hand, and turned to leave the room.

"Let me help you with the Bezzos problem," the Speaker offered as Tibideaux reached the door. "Okay?"

Tibideaux paused for a moment and then replied, "Yes, Sir. Thank you." He didn't want the Leader's help with Bezzos because that would only give Bezzos more ammunition. Matthew wanted to fight his own fight, but he also didn't want to irritate the Leader. There was too much at stake here.

Once outside in the hallway, he placed a call to Fred Ming Yao. "Hello?" Fred answered.

"Matthew here. We need to meet soon. I have some good news."

"That is good, my friend," Yao replied. "How about next Tuesday? You should leave the evening free for dinner and celebration. Shall I bring the package?"

"Absolutely," Tibideaux replied. "Tuesday is good. When and where?"

"Seven p.m. at The Willows in Maryland."

"See you then."

A few days later, Mr. Yao's driver picked him up and drove him to the meeting place. Gunter, the driver, was a solidly built man whose bald head glistened in the glow of the streetlights. He wore a cheap suit with the hint of a tattoo showing slightly above his shirt collar. He was Mr. Yao's bodyguard and took his assignment seriously. He was also Mr. Yao's chauffeur. The senator had often wondered what the tattoo was but had been afraid to ask.

At the restaurant, Tibideaux got out of the car, looking quickly left and right. There was no one he recognized on the street, so he entered the restaurant and saw that his dinner companions were already at the table. Fred Ming Yao rose from his chair as the senator approached.

"Good evening, Senator," he said, bowing slightly and extending his hand with the polite formality of a Chinese stereotype. He was well-groomed and very conservatively dressed.

"Good evening, good evening," the senator smiled, grasping Yao's hand with a slight bow of his own.

"Senator," Mr. Yao continued, "you remember Ms. Guifei?"

"Certainly," Matthew replied, extending his hand as his eyes traveled over her well-muscled body, wrapped tightly in a form-fitting yellow dress which accentuated her supple breasts. Her jet-black hair was expertly coiffed around her face. "How could I forget one of the 'four beauties'?" he asked, referring to the Chinese folk tale about the four most beautiful women in Chinese history. Yang Guifei, one of the four, was reported to have lived during the Tang Dynasty. It was said that she had "a face that would make all flowers feel shameful." His eyes traveled once more over her body. *This one could make my flower stand up and take notice with no shame whatsoever.*

Sue Yang Guifei recognized his glance and felt a warm wave of pride. She knew the effect she could have on men and was proud of

31

it. "Nice to see you again," she said, coquettishly lowering her eyes while allowing him to take her hand.

Sue Guifei was truly a beautiful woman and moved with the grace of the athlete she had once been. Born to parents who were both poor factory workers, she had somehow caught the attention of Chinese backers of the Chinese Olympics Committee. She had been taken from a local school yard and offered a chance to train at a prominent facility. At first, she cried to stay with her family, but her parents had told her it was for her own good. Tears filled her eyes as she remembered their last goodbye. She had done well in training and participated in numerous international events, including being named as an alternate for the Chinese Olympic Gymnastics team. Her specialty had been the floor routine where she exhibited suppleness and grace. Thereafter she was recruited by Chinese Intelligence to help China achieve world dominance. She'd been schooled in accounting and was subsequently assigned to a unit based in the United States to work with Fred Ming Yao.

They were meeting at The Willows Restaurant and Tavern, a cozy restaurant with a friendly, but not pushy wait staff. The Willows is located about one hour's drive south of the nation's capitol and the clientele is mostly local, and quiet. It was also outside of the senator's normal play area, which minimized his risk of being recognized. The food was excellent and the senator, who always enjoyed a good meal, ordered the evening's special – Tarragon Scallops and the Pork Umbria.

"And how was your meeting?" Yao asked.

"Excellent," he replied. "You are assured of getting the contract."

Fred Yao was the president of Yao Enterprises, a software firm that had been doing business with several of Louisiana's state agencies, as well as the United States National Aeronautics and

Space Administration. The Senator was the company's primary lobbyist and had been handsomely rewarded for the business he had been able to steer to Mr. Yao and his company. As a lobbyist, the senator knew how to use his influence. He was mostly cordial in his business dealings, but people with whom he dealt knew that he was a powerful political figure and were reluctant to argue with him. On occasion, however, he had firmly reminded some individuals who he was and the power he could exercise if they did not support his efforts.

Like most politicians, Marshall Tibideaux had not started out corrupt, but as the saying goes, "power corrupts and absolute power corrupts absolutely." He also needed to build his campaign chest for whatever political position he decided to pursue in the future. He'd grown up in Louisiana as a bright young man and everyone who knew him predicted a great future for him. Even then, he knew how to make and to use connections. He hadn't come to Washington as a corrupt politician, but once he'd begun accepting the various "gifts," it became impossible to turn back. It had been easy to rationalize what he was doing. Tibideaux seldom thought about the first time he had accepted a gift and each time that he did, it seemed less and less an error in judgment. Additionally, each time he accepted a bribe, he was able to do some small favor for the citizens of Louisiana and was rewarded with more accolades. The "thank you" and the "Oh, you are so wonderful for our state," and the other accolades were not only very gratifying, but as they came more and more frequently, they helped to blot out the memories of his cowardice. It was a nice feeling. He felt it was the respect he rightfully deserved.

Early in his career he had stepped in to add his voice and influence to a state construction project by secretly calling two of the state officials on the board and advising them that he favored a certain contractor over the others in the bidding. His recommendation was the deciding factor and his choice received a lucrative contract. A short time later, the contract recipient had come to see him, bringing an envelope filled with money.

"Oh, I can't accept that," Tibideaux protested mildly.

"But Senator," the recipient insisted, "What you did was good for the state. I am the best choice. You did the right thing. This could help your re-election campaign. No one will ever know."

Reluctantly, the Senator accepted the money. Using his influence was much easier after that – and usually more rewarding. He convinced himself that it really was okay. After all, everyone in Washington was on the take somehow. *At least, I'm not on some madam's call list, using the money to buy sex for my own pleasure. Something good happens for my state and my constituents because of this. I'm one of the good guys. I AM COLOSSUS! I right wrongs and punish the guilty! Louisiana and the country need me!*

"Wonderful news," Sue replied. "This will be important for our next quarterly forecast. I think it is about time for us to consider an expansion into some of the larger U.S. companies. I, for one, would like to develop some greater ties with Boeing, Lockheed, and other aviation-related companies."

She produced a set of papers with financial forecasts, options, and recommendations. One look at the papers and the senator could see how precise and professional her preparations were. She was also quite articulate and logical.

Damn, she's good, thought Matthew, impressed with her command of the company financials. She truly did have an understanding of the business. Yao had always presented her as the Chief Financial Officer, but the senator had virtually ignored this information because he was convinced that she was merely Yao's mistress. *Maybe she's good at both,* he chuckled to himself. He was momentarily distracted from her briefing as he mentally undressed her.

"Senator?" Sue addressed him twice before he responded.

"Oh, I agree," he responded quickly.

Sue smiled at him knowingly, then closed her books and handed an envelope to Yao.

It was shortly after seven when they finished dinner. "And now I believe it is time to celebrate," Yao proclaimed. "Senator, if you will be so kind as to accompany us." Yao rose and proceeded out of the restaurant with Gunter following immediately behind him. Matthew moved quickly to assist Sue with her chair. She thanked him and then turned as she left so that their bodies touched ever so gently as she walked by, producing an electric tingling in his lower body.

"Thank you," she said, smiling, "and goodnight."

"Aren't you coming with us?" he inquired.

"Oh, no. I still have work to do. Enjoy." Again, she flashed him a knowing smile. "Perhaps next time I can celebrate with you."

"I'll look forward to that," he replied with a smile.

Gunter retrieved the car and waited in front of the restaurant. Yao and the senator sat in back. They carried on a polite conversation, but mostly listened to the soft music of a local station. Gunter drove them back into the city to an exclusive hotel not far from Capitol hill. En route they drove past the U.S. Capitol Building. Tibideaux always felt a sense of awe when he viewed the Capitol, but his awe was even stronger at night. The Capitol Building is a great symbol of America and of the ideals of our Founding Fathers. A beautiful example of 19th century neo-classical architecture, the polished Georgian marble fairly glows in the moonlight.

There was a slight breeze. Tibideaux caught a glimpse of the four American flags waving gently in the night. He knew that the two center flags have flown continuously, day and night, since World War I. The other two fly over the respective wings for the Senate and the House of Representatives, but only when they are in session.

Beautiful, the senator thought, marveling at the display of lights on the white marble walls. He laughed, recalling the story of several years back when a U.S. Congressman had been caught having sex behind one of the pillars on the Capitol steps. The woman he was with happened to be his wife and everyone in the know had a good laugh. The congressman received only a mild reprimand and was forgiven by his constituents; however, they were angered when he was later convicted of accepting bribes. Still, Congressmen and women forgive their own.

Inside the hotel, they walked to the elevator. Gunter checked to ensure the elevator was empty and quickly ushered Yao and the senator inside. Upstairs, they hurried to a private suite. Yao and Matthew entered and Gunter left on an errand.

"Nice place," Tibideaux commented, surveying the suite. It had a magnificent view of the city bustling below.

"Yes, thank you. Would you like a drink?" Yao asked. Matthew nodded and Yao poured them both a drink from the well-stocked bar. Then, reaching into his suit pocket, Yao produced the envelope Sue had given him at the restaurant – "the package" and handed it to the senator, who for one moment held it in one hand as if weighing the contents. "It's all there," Yao assured him with a smile. "But you should count it for yourself."

"Not necessary," Matthew replied, "I trust you." He placed the envelope and the $50,000 it contained into his inside suit pocket. This was only one of many such transactions they had conducted over the past two years totaling nearly $250,000. All of it had been passed covertly, with no way to trace it. There was a knock at the door.

"Come in," Yao announced.

Gunter opened the door and led two women into the room. Both had the makings of being attractive women and their attire suggested that the "celebration party" was about to begin. The older woman went immediately to the bar and poured drinks for both of them. The younger one focused her attention on the senator, sizing him up and then smiled her approval. The senator smiled back, and the party began.

The older woman finished her drink in one quick motion and then found a soft and sensuous music station. "Wanna dance?" she asked, wrapping herself around him like a tortilla around the meat in an enchilada.

She began to move with the music – a slow, sultry, sensuous motion. As they danced, the younger woman lit a reefer, took a long drag, and then molded her body in behind him. *She's the pico de gallo*, he thought. He liked it a lot. The three of them danced this way for a few minutes and when the music stopped, the younger woman offered him a drag on her reefer. He inhaled deeply. *Wow! Top grade stuff!*

Yao quietly sipped his drink, while Gunter stood guard at the door.

"C'mon, join in," the senator urged.

"No, thank you," Yao replied. "Enjoy. This is your party."

The women alternated the front and back positions. The one in front continually offered Matthew alcohol and marijuana, which he readily accepted. Soon, he began to stagger as he danced and found it difficult to stay focused. He giggled like a little boy as his hands explored each of these women.

Eventually, they took him into the bedroom and began to undress him. He wanted to take charge and to show them that "he

37

was the man," but the combination of marijuana and alcohol was too strong, so he laid down like a big, docile puppy dog while the women treated him to a variety of sexual pleasures, though bestowed with disdain. They were professionals and knew that their payday was in the hands of the Asian guy in the other room – and if he wanted the senator to be pleased, they would please the senator. One of them opened a small packet of cocaine. They alternated taking hits and servicing the senator until he passed out. They left him sprawled across the expansive bed and went to collect their money. They offered to service the Oriental guy, but he politely refused and gave them their money.

Gunter took the senator back to his apartment and put him to bed. The senator did not make it to "the Hill in time to cast his vote on the new military appropriations bill; however, he was sufficiently recovered in time to attend the evening festivities at a fundraising party.

"Thank you for coming," Senator Tibideux addressed the assemblage of wealthy businessmen and Party faithful. "As your senator from the great state of Louisiana and one of your elected representatives in Congress, let me speak to you tonight about the moral and ethical climate in our nation's capital. It is imperative that we, the elected representatives, adhere to the tenets and ethics of our Founding Fathers. We must say what we mean and mean what we say." Recalling his vision of the Capitol Building the previous evening, he added. "Each time I behold the sight of our beautiful Capitol Building, I am filled with a great joy, knowing that I have the opportunity to walk in the footsteps of great men. Know this, I will not let you down... and as a personal note, I believe that we should also follow the mandates of Christianity – both in our working lives and in our personal lives."

He was interrupted by a burst of applause. Inwardly, he smiled. *I'm good at the impromptu additions.* He continued speaking for another thirty minutes, striking all the chords and using all of the buzz words of a polished politician. He knew his audience well and played them accordingly. He was interrupted several times by resounding applause. By the time he finished, he was the sentimental front-runner for the governorship of the great state of Louisiana or a strong favorite to retain his Senate seat – whichever way he chose to run.

New Orleans, Louisiana

Back in Louisiana, as the senator partied and played politics, his family was following their normal routine. The maid was preparing dinner. Nadine, his eighteen year-old daughter was texting all of her school friends. This was her senior year and she was excited about graduating and going to LSU. As the captain of the school's Cheerleading Squad, she was immensely popular. She also had a knack for reaching out to new students arriving at the school. "We should make everyone feel welcome here," she bubbled to anyone and everyone. "Put yourself in their shoes," she would argue. "Have to leave your old friends, go someplace new, and be all alone. That'd be terrible."

"Yeah, she's just like her dad – a politician," someone muttered.

"Hush," her friends replied. "At least she tries to help others. You just sit on your butt and complain."

"Fuck you," the first one replied and walked away.

Gary, Matthew's fifteen year-old son, was playing video games. He had a few friends, but was basically a loner. He had none of his father's charming ways, although he desperately wanted them. Physically, he was very similar. Already six feet tall, he was well-proportioned, but his walk gave him away – even before his faltering speech. He had no self-confidence. It was as if his sister had inherited it all of their father's admirable attributes and he was convinced that both parents loved her more than they loved him. His was a lonely life.

Nicole Tibideaux was upstairs in her office going over the company books. Her father had founded a chain of seafood and Creole restaurants around the state, starting in New Orleans. The first restaurant had been destroyed by a fire but never rebuilt. Instead he'd built others and they'd been hugely successful.

Inasmuch as she was an only child, Nicole had inherited the family business when her father died. Under any circumstance, she would have been the logical choice. Her parents had put her to work waiting tables for the evening meals when she was only nine. She'd learned the business well and she was frugal. She still had her first waitressing tip wrapped in a small napkin and tucked away in her dresser – all sixty-five cents of it! She'd worked at the restaurant ever since and at eighteen when her friends went off to college she became the manager of one of her daddy's restaurants.

By the time her friends had graduated and were looking for jobs, she was an established business success. She even hired a few of them to wait tables while circulating their resumes for "professional" positions. Initially, she had been excited and had hoped that Matthew would help her run the company, but he was not interested in such mundane work; however, he'd been more than happy to enjoy the comfort of his wife's money since he had very little of his own. She was an excellent business person and had hired several very capable managers who enjoyed the considerable latitude she gave them in operating the restaurants. Her only real demand was that her father's recipe for seafood gumbo be prominently featured as the house specialty.

She hadn't been too happy with Matthew's decision to run for senator because it meant a lot of family separation, but he'd promised her that he would schedule his workload so as to be home at least three weekends a month. He had kept his word. He would normally fly home early Friday afternoon and return to Washington early Monday morning. This meant that his attendance record on the floor of the senate would not be the best example, but not bad enough to call serious attention to his failings. Besides, he was only holding the prospect of a second term as a fall-back position because he was looking to the governorship.

The intercom light on Nicole's desk lit up. She heard the maid's voice. "Ma'am, dinner is ready."

"Thanks, please call the kids."

"Well, how was your day?" Nicole asked the kids when they were all seated at the dining table.

"Bout the same," Nadine replied. Gary grunted something undecipherable.

"Look," Nicole suggested, "how about a big barbecue when your dad comes home this weekend? You can invite your friends."

"Sure," Nadine replied. Gary grunted again. Basically, he didn't have any friends to invite, so it really didn't matter to him.

"Great, then that's what we'll do."

Early the next morning, as the senator slept off his hangover in the nation's capital, Nicole began preparing for the weekend. The house had a large porch outside of the kitchen, with a superb barbecue grill. In the summer, the porch was screened in to keep the Louisiana bugs out while allowing a lovely breeze to flow around the house. At the right time, the breeze carried with it the fragrance of exotic flowers. In the winter, it was enclosed in glass which provided a breathtaking view across the lawn, then down past a small lake. It was an ideal arrangement.

The maid cleaned and straightened the lower floor rooms while Nicole called several close friends and church members, inviting them to their family cook-out after church. Nicole was happy. She had a nice home, two lovely children, a thriving business, and a successful husband who loved her. She'd watched his speech on the political channel and was thrilled at how handsome and composed he appeared.

As the Tibideaux family gathered for the Sunday barbecue, Fred Ming Yao was on an international flight headed for Beijing, China to attend a meeting with the Chinese Intelligence Service where he would report on the status of China's breach of the United States' national defense systems.

Four

"Beijing, China"

Fred Ming Yao left the Beijing Airport and breathed deeply. It was good to be home again. The air seemed alive. *American air is polluted, like acid. It is good to breathe the air of my own country.*

He hailed a cab and went to his hotel. It was late. He'd been traveling for almost three days and he was extremely tired. He had two days to rest until his meeting and he needed every minute of that time.

After a good night's sleep, Yao spent the day enjoying the sights and sounds of his homeland. He even walked past the building where he'd built his first company. *It has not changed much, but I have.* Memories of his youth made him smile.

"Why do you never take a break?" His father asked. "Even Confucius, who praised diligence, has said that 'to go beyond is as wrong as to fall short,' you work too hard. Come, have some tea."

Fred replied, "Confucius also said that 'Wheresoever you go, go with all your heart.' I intend to be a successful business man, and so, must work with all my heart." His father had left, shaking his head. "Tea will be waiting when you come home."

It was pleasant to hear people around him speaking Chinese; and the food! He had not found a decent Chinese restaurant anywhere in Washington, D.C. In Beijing his options were limitless. Yes, it was good to be home.

"Good morning, sir." A good looking young man, smartly wearing the uniform of a junior officer in the Chinese People's Liberation Army greeted Yao as he entered the People's Library Building. Inside, he was taken to an impressive looking conference room where the walls were covered with rare paintings of Chinese history. Beautiful red banners hung from the ceiling and the conference table was of the finest Rosewood, polished to an exquisite sheen. Yao smiled. It was so much more civilized than his meetings with the American representatives. Their conference rooms all spoke of great wealth, but none of them compared to the Chinese conference rooms, which spoke to the richness of life and the traditions of the Chinese people.

"Thank you all for coming." The speaker was a senior official of the Chinese Intelligence Service (ChIS). "This meeting is vital to our national security. It is important that each of you understand your role and responsibility in our ongoing operations. It is also imperative that you recognize the great need for security in each segment of this operation." The participants all nodded in agreement.

"We are involved in a global war to determine which nation will be dominant in the next decade. This war has not been declared as such, but, none the less - it is a war. At the present time, Americans still think theirs is the most powerful nation in the world. The truth, however; is that, today, it is merely a façade. America has slipped considerably over the past thirty years and it is nearing the time for us to expose its weaknesses, and bring it to its knees. In the long history of man, the powerful nations have established the rules, both for peace and for war. The world is weary of America making the rules. It is time for us to make the rules. We will capitalize on the weaknesses of the American people and of their government. There are three major areas for us to know and to attack.

"First, they are an arrogant, impatient and lazy people. They believe no other nation can equal them, and they are in denial over the facts of their diminishing power, yet, the rest of the world can see it. They have grown "soft" as a people. They are no longer that "greatest generation" that could withstand hardships and survive and even win. They have not won a war for over seventy years. They do not have the stomach for war unless they can win quickly, but they are too weak, morally, to win quickly. Although their soldiers seem to be of good quality, their political leaders will not allow them to fight to win. And, it appears most of their generals and admirals have become like the snake – shedding their skins. They have shed the skin of the warrior to now wear the skin of the politician. Their politicians are too afraid of being 'politically incorrect' to take decisive and adequate action. They piece-meal their warfare. One of my favorite books is the autobiography of General Giap, the commander of the North Vietnamese Army that defeated the Americans in Vietnam. In his book, he states clearly that twice America had the North Vietnamese beaten; they were ready to surrender, and then the American politicians took the victory away from the American soldiers. To his death, he was puzzled by such stupidity. We must provide every opportunity for them to face a crisis—exhibit this stupidity - and fail. We do not need for the crisis to be a major event, only enough to show their indecisiveness.

"Second, today, the common people expect their government to provide for everything. They cannot handle hardship. As a nation, they are becoming weak from within. If it snows in their cities, they cry and blame the government – rather than step outside and shovel themselves free. Their education system is now one of the lowest of the industrial nations. They do not feel the need to work for an education: after all, their government will even give them free phones! If they are not willing to work to feed their families, they will not fight to preserve their freedoms. They are a weak people. They are mostly beggars. We must help to expedite this growing weakness. Actually, they are destroying themselves with their 'entitlement attitude'; we are merely speeding up the process of destruction.

"Third, economically, they are still living off of the power and foresight of their "greatest" generation, yet they no longer respect that generation. A great number of them are incapable of working for a living; they only want the handout from others – either their government, or something. Recently, the International Monetary Fund informed the world that our economy will be number one in the world within the next few years. We will replace America as the greatest economy in the world. The entire world sees the weaknesses of America – except the Americans.

"We will destroy them by following the precepts of 'unrestricted warfare'. This concept was developed and published by two senior officers of the People's Liberation Army, in the 1990's. It requires us to exploit every facet of life: to rethink the concepts of warfare. Warfare no longer means merely the exercise of military power. We are now attacking them successfully in the economic arena. We have established a balance of trade that is very much in our favor. And, it will only get better.   "There are two primary reasons for this: One, as mentioned earlier, the common people expect their government to provide for them and they are not willing to work as did their 'greatest' generation. Secondly, their wealthy are only interested in more wealth and will cater to our 'cheap labor.' We are also the largest holder of their national debt. When the time is right we will call it due and bankrupt them. For now, however, we need them. They are no longer the 'greatest generation,' but they are the 'greatest consumers.'" The assembled participants laughed at the thought of the pathetic Americans who could no longer produce anything of value, but bought anything available – with borrowed money.

"But, rest assured," he continued. "The time will come – and soon. For now, we still need for them to borrow money from us and to buy our goods. It helps our workers to enjoy a better life. The Russians are working with us to remove the American dollar as the world's reserve currency. Additionally, some of the oil producing countries no longer accept the dollar as the currency for trade of oil. The many cards of the American Empire are about to fall."

"Excuse me, Sir. But, don't we still need them to buy our goods?" asked an attendee.

"Yes," he replied. "But soon, that will not be necessary. We are attacking them physically and surreptitiously through the use of our Muslim allies. It is through the Muslim allies that we exercise the most effective military actions without exposing any of our own people. We merely supply money — money which the Americans give us. Ironic isn't it? They buy our goods and give us money, which we can then use to supply Muslim armies and terrorists to attack them!" There was a low murmuring of laughter, accompanied by a nodding of heads.

"The Americans are afraid of the Muslims. Also, there are a number of their politicians who, for money, advocate for Islam, under the guise of freedom. In the near future, there will be a number of attacks in multiple cities within the United States, spurred by the Jihadists – and largely performed by American citizens who have converted to Islam. It is an interesting phenomenon, how naïve – or cowardly – the American people are.

Recently, someone announced that the Islamists have nuclear bombs buried all across America. The American news media – and many people- said that was ridiculous – not possible. "Science fiction," many said. They do not remember that their own army had small tactical nuclear weapons in mass production in the 1950's. It was called the 'Davey Crockett'; named after one of their heroes. Small enough for one man to carry; powerful enough to destroy one U.S city block. Also, easy to hide, or bury. But, Americans do not read history, and, thus do not learn from it.

The People's Republic will be quick to offer condolences and even aid and assistance. We will denounce terrorist acts and to the world we will be seen as a compassionate people, desiring only peace and good will. This will be important in the area of public opinion. Whatever course of action they take in response to the attacks inside their homeland, we will make them appear foolish in the eyes of the world. If they respond with force, we will help the world to condemn them for excessive force. If they do not respond, we will portray them as too weak to continue as the world's leader. Either way, they will be so divided internally, that they will appear foolish.

We have already seen this in their responses to North Korea. Each time North Korea acts against South Korea, the world looks to see what will be the American response. So far, the American response has actually been one of "no response." North Korea attacks the south and kills many people. The United States response is to do a harmless dance that they call 'military maneuvers.' The only thing missing from their dance is their tutu." Laughter filled the room. "The world sees them as a 'paper tiger'- and, toothless at that."

"Yes," someone offered. "Imagine their President and their Secretary of State wearing 'tutus' and dancing to Swan Lake!" More laughter.

"Actually," someone yelled, "to see their Secretary of State in a tutu would be a frightening sight! Let us hope they never actually do get to them." Still more laughter.

"Yes," the speaker continued. "The world can see that their world power is diminishing. They cannot use force to assist their allies for fear we will also use force. They are no longer the dominant military power in the world – mostly because they do not understand how to use power. But, they like to pose as dominant. We will continue to allow them to do so – for the time.

"And, our other Muslim allies are of great value. Iran has assisted us in providing weapons to the Taliban. Soon, America will withdraw from Afghanistan. They will do so with a great show, and a 'declaration of victory,' but, the world will know it is just another case of taking on something too big for their weak mental capabilities – and then quitting before the effort can be completed. This is not the America of the 1940's and 1950's. Finally, Iran is working with Venezuela and placing missiles there that will be capable of striking American cities – and these missiles can be outfitted to carry nuclear warheads.

"Excuse me, Sir," a young man asked. "How, exactly, are we directing the Muslims to attack?"

"An excellent question...and an important one. We do not direct them in any way. We merely supply money as needed. The radical Muslims can attack in any manner they choose. If we are not giving instructions, we cannot be blamed if anything goes awry. And any action they take against America will do harm to America, and thus, improve our position vis-à-vis the Americans. It is what Americans like to call a 'win-win' situation.

"We must also attack them through technology. That is why you are so important. You are all to be congratulated for the many classified documents and the technological information you have taken from them, thus, allowing us to be ahead of them in their space and communications endeavors. I do wish to caution you to remain unobtrusive. In the honored words of Sun Tzu, from his writings *The Art of War:* 'Be so subtle that you are invisible. Be so mysterious that you are intangible. Then you will control your rival's fate.'

"Also, remember that our greatest successes, both in America and in Canada have been through identifying and bribing the corrupt bureaucrats and politicians. Bureaucrats and politicians since the beginning of time have been corrupt, but Americans have developed corruption into an art form, especially with their ability to rationalize and to turn their corruption into a badge of honor. And, of course, their news media are largely self-serving lap-dogs for the corrupt politicians. They only further confuse any given issue; but we do not wish to denigrate their news media. Their liberal journalists are perhaps our greatest allies, albeit, unknowingly. They use many big words, but they are basically not very intelligent. I once heard an American expression, which I did not understand at the time but now I do. It goes like this, 'An American journalist can – with all seriousness — debate and rationalize how to pick up a 'turd' by the clean end.'"

Laughter was sprinkled throughout the room, but was interrupted by one person raising their hand and asking, "Excuse me sir. I do not understand. What is a 'turd'?"

"Oh, certainly," the speaker smiled. "A 'turd' is American slang for feces – either the human kind, or from a dog."

"Oh," the questioner replied," grinning broadly, while nodding that he now understood the joke.

The speaker continued. "Your government appreciates the fine work that you are doing and expects you to continue. Thank you."

The participants applauded and then were each asked to present their reports on the challenges they had encountered, how they had managed to overcome these challenges and what were the results of their efforts.

Yao's presentation was strikingly similar to those which had preceded him. "Money and sex are the keys to the American politician," he began. "Most of them already have power. Now they want the accoutrements that they feel should go with that power. It is imperative; however, that they believe their participation is merely part of a commercial venture. If they once realize that their corruption could harm their national security, many – but not all — become what, in their slang, they call 'flaky'. For some, the lure of sex and money are still overpowering, but most will balk once they believe that they have become only traitors. Of course, by the time they figure it out, it is usually too late. Once their brains have fallen into their groin, they cannot recover."

Yao was interrupted by the nodding of agreement by the participants. He smiled and thought to himself, *It was a good joke.*

"Most of all," he continued, "these traitors are in a state of denial. Some of their psychologists would say it is a form of cognitive dissonance – they cannot believe that they are so weak; their minds keep telling them that they are the heroes. They cannot accept that they are doing harm. When exposed, they mostly, denounce those who expose them. Depending on how much power they have, usually the denouncers are more ridiculed and denigrated than are the corrupt politicians. This is especially true in their federal government. It is not uncommon for them to choose as the head of any ethics inquiries – the very ones amongst them who most violate their ethics. America will fall from within – we must merely assist – and, then be ready to capitalize on their fall. But, back to the subject.

"Once they recognize what they are doing, you must get rid of them – and quickly. At that moment, not only are they no longer of value, but they can become a danger – especially, if they decide to tell all to their authorities."

Yao also explained how he had used contacts and money supplied by the Shanghai Triad, one of many Chinese mafia style organizations, to build his company. The initial bribe of the Louisiana Senator had come from this triad.

"Excuse me. Allow me to clarify." The host speaker stepped beside Yao. "The Triads," he began, "have established many legitimate businesses around the world which serve as conduits for many nationalistic covert operations, as well as for Chinese Intelligence gathering, their contribution to the security of the Chinese people has been recognized by the highest levels of our government."

He explained how the success of the various triads in Canada had established considerable control over life in Canada, resulting in the compromise of some Canadian policies and adding to the security of the Chinese people. He encouraged all participants to explore the possibility of developing triad activities within the scope of their own businesses, and then he allowed Yao to continue. Yao explained that his involvement with the Shanghai Triad had been modeled on the Canadian operations. "It is also a very lucrative partnership," he informed them, "and relatively safe and easy. Most Americans do not even know the Triads exist; those who do know do not seem to care."

As the day concluded, Yao was approached by a senior member of ChIS. "Mr. Yao," he said, "please come with me. We have a special mission for you."

Across town, Yao was ushered into a top secret compound and introduced to a lady named Jinjing Wu, identified as the leader of a critical research group. "It is my pleasure to meet you," she began. I have heard wonderful things about your work. But, we have a special mission for you."

"And what would that be," Yao asked.

"We understand that you will be receiving a contract for work with the American NASA. Is that correct?"

"Yes."

"Good. We are currently working on a project to build a computer virus to attack America's infrastructure. Have you heard of the Stuxnet virus that did such harm to the Iranian nuclear program?"

"No."

"Well, you will hear more. Just listen to the American news media. They will be discussing it. You can assist us greatly by identifying the manufacturer of all the NASA components you encounter – by any means possible. Can you do that?"

"Surely, once the contract is final, I should have very good access."

"Good. We look forward to your results. When do you think that will be?"

"The contracts are tentatively scheduled for completion in less than a year. I will try to get my source to expedite – but at most eighteen months until I can implement. Then probably another six months to get into their system. So, all told – two years at most."

"Wonderful," she said, smiling. "The beautiful aspect of this new program lies in the Americans not understanding the changing world. They are still looking for spies who are trying to steal their secrets. With this new computer virus, we do not care about their secrets. The world of cyber warfare has changed all the dynamics. Once we introduce the virus, their IT and communications systems will be rendered inoperable whenever we decide to execute. We are preparing to put something *into* their system while they are trying to keep us from *taking anything out*. They are easy to deceive, these Americans," she said, and left the room.

Yao returned to the scheduled meeting, which lasted three additional days and then he returned to the United States. All of his papers were, naturally, in order and he entered the U.S. with no incidents or delays. His latest contracts would allow him to gain access to many of America's most highly guarded secrets within NASA and the FAA. Such information would be most valuable to Chinese Intelligence and for the status of his country, for space will be a tremendous force in the conduct of future wars. This information would also be valuable in the growing "cyber-wars" being conducted by all nations. Soon, China would be able to cripple U.S. military satellite operations at will. The next step would be gaining the ability to attack U.S. infrastructure, such as power grids and water systems. *When we decide to attack, it will be relatively easy,* he grinned. He returned with a light heart. He was doing a service for his country. Although his part was only a small one in the overall scheme of things he was recognized for doing it well. And, he was becoming wealthy for doing so, which did not diminish his pride. He was doing quite well for one whose parents had been simple farmers.

Five

"From Sea to Shining Sea: Activity Across America"

Castaic, California

"Hey, thanks for having us all over." Jim Birdwell extended his hand.

"No sweat. Everybody needs a break now and then." Danny Cavuto replied, stoking the coals on the grill. "Good to get all the neighbors together."

"Yeah, hell, might not be able to do this pretty soon, the way the economy is goin'," Ben Smith added. "Think we're gonna be the first generation where our kids live less well than we did? Why can't we get rid of these crooked politicians?"

The others shook their heads and replied, sadly, "Because they are all crooked. No matter who replaces whom. They are all bad, or become bad."

"Yeah," Ben offered. "I think it was Thomas Jefferson who said: 'My reading of history convinces me that most bad government results from too much government.'"

"Amen," Birdwell responded. "And it is our own fault. We have become a nation of beggars – everybody thinks the government owes them a hand-out.

"Wait a minute," Will Smart spoke up. "Not everyone. Damn it, I bust my ass and I pay my taxes – so don't say everyone."

"Okay, but, you know what I mean. Hell, damn near forty percent of Americans are on some form of welfare. Right?" There was a nodding of heads and then Birdwell continued. "What we need are more people willing to work and pay taxes. And to take accountability for what we do as individuals. The politicians didn't just dream up the housing bubble – we, the people, drove them to it. We need to take some accountability as a people."

"That's a pipe-dream," Ben responded. "You're right, it ain't just the politicians. A people always get the government they deserve – that's the history of the world. And, that is exactly what we are getting. I agree, our politicians are probably the worst the world has ever seen—but, after all, aren't they representative of the population? Don't they represent us? We need to stop talking about how politicians need to be accountable. Instead, we need to start showing some accountability ourselves. We need to revive the Tea Party groups. And, this time we need to bring guns."

Will interrupted. "Hey, don't be talkin' out in the open 'bout guns and shit. 'Big Brother' will snatch your ass up in a hurry. Hell, send the Gestapo after all of us. Be Careful how you talk, OK?"

"Yeah, you're right. But, it's tough as hell to stay fired up. I guess we are going to have to take a real hard time to get enough folks fired up again. We are a corrupt society, and so we get corrupt politicians. Too many people out there won't give up suckin' on the hind tit of 'free government money'. And now the crooked politicians know how to buy their votes. It's our own damn fault. We are too damn complacent, and it is going to cost us big time. When all this spending and debt comes due, a lot of folks will be going hungry who never had to before – and some will die. It is going to get nasty. You think those riots in Europe were bad – just wait! Remember New Orleans after that hurricane? People didn't try to help themselves; all they did was blame the government for not helping. Compare that to the Japanese after the 'quake and tsunami. Hell, they didn't cry, they just worked at fixing things. Americans can't do that anymore."

"Yeah." Birdwell added. "Look at Detroit. In the last ten years, nearly one-quarter of the people living there have left. People believed the big promises of the politicians and labor big-wigs – and the city went to hell. Sometimes, you can't vote the bums out, so you vote with your feet – and move somewhere else."

"Yeah, and I think that guy who wrote the book *Shadow Government* is on to something. That rich old bastard, George Soros has bought most of the politicians in America. We are about to become just another "third world socialist country."

"Hey!" Cavuto shouted. "We all decided to have a cook-out, drink some beer, and relax. Not to discuss politics. Now, knock it off, or I'm just gonna turn the beer keg over and water my lawn with it! Unless you knock this shit off!"

"Hey, don't waste the beer!" Someone laughed. "I'll shut up!"

"Me, too!" The others all responded.

Washington, DC

The chairman of the U.S. Congressional House Ways and Means Committee met privately with lawyers from the ACLU.

"Well," the chairman asked. "Did you deposit the money?"

The head of the ACLU delegation nodded.

"So, is there anything else to discuss here?" the Chairman asked.

"Just that you better hold up your end of the deal," the lawyer replied.

"Oh, I will, I will," the Chairman replied.

"Just be sure you do."

They shook hands and the lawyers left.

The Chairman leaned back in his chair, lit a cigar and smiled. *The American way*, he thought, *I scratch their back; they scratch mine - and I get a little something for myself*. He checked his watch. He had ordered the newest intern to come see him at 2:30. *She's a cute little thing with really big tits. I hope she's agile*.

New Orleans

Johnny Bezzos clicked his remote and turned the TV on to his favorite channel, Fox News.

"Good evening, and welcome to Fox News," the announcer proclaimed. "Tonight we'll be showing some frightening videos concerning the growth of America's internal jihad threat. You will see actual videos of Islamic Jihad training compounds. There are known to be at least thirty-five such compounds across America. They call themselves 'The Soldiers of Allah' and they are engaged in paramilitary training, which involves guns, explosives and bombs, and hand-to-hand combat training. The group is led by a known Islamic terrorist living in Pakistan. They will not allow the news media to interview any of the participants or to film any of the activities.

"Why does our government allow such activities? When we investigate these activities, we are told that they are protected by the U.S. Constitution. This begs the question: Do our laws require us to protect the very people who intend to do us harm? Evidently, yes."

"Honey," Melinda pleaded. "Can't we spend just one day without listening to more news? I know you like Fox, but it's always the same old garbage."

"Well, I'm damn sure not gonna watch anything on MSNBC."

"I know," she moaned, "but I'm tired of all of them. Doesn't anybody have any good news?"

Johnny changed the channels until he found an old war movie. "This looks good. How 'bout some popcorn?"

Melinda's eyes rolled as she shook her head and left the room. "Call me when you find something we can both watch."

Six

"The Business of Washington"

The Offices of the Department of Homeland Security

"Tell me more about this Stuxnet virus." John Adamson, the Secretary of Homeland Security, was curious.

"Well, Sir," the briefer began, "we really know very little about it, but it's real. The level of sophistication is the highest of any computer virus we've ever seen. It's also an extensive program. We estimate that it's traveled most of the world, just waiting for an opportunity to hit the intended target. We are convinced that it required some governmental involvement – maybe multiple governments. Our first inclination was to believe that it had originated in Israel. The Israelis had both motive and the brain-power to conduct this operation. Yet, when we ask them about it all they do is grin and shake their heads. If they did produce it, they aren't telling anyone... but they had motive and capability."

"Tell me again how it worked." The Secretary leaned toward the screen.

"Well, Sir," the briefer continued, "it was designed to attack a specific piece of hardware. Some operative determined the manufacturer of the key centrifuges needed for Iran to successfully build an atomic weapon. Turns out it was the German manufacturer, Siemens, who built the centrifuge. The virus was built to attack these specific machines. It was introduced into the Iranian national computer network until it found the target. It was able to travel the world through many different computers. The interesting part is that it stays undetected and actually does no harm until it finds the intended target. Chances are, half of the personal computers right here in America have the "bug" and don't realize it. Maybe even you – or you kids – have the bug on your personal computers. Actually, I wouldn't be surprised if it isn't in most of the iphone apps everyone has. It's harmless – except for the specified target. The damn thing is the most sophisticated virus we have ever seen."

"Yeah, but once it finds the target, I understand it's extremely effective," added the Secretary. "I hope you all realize that this is a real game-changer. This is the first ever, true cyber terrorist threat at this level."

"Yes, Sir, we do. Once it infiltrated Iran's nuclear production facilities, it wreaked havoc. We estimate it set back the Iranian nuclear production program by at least six months, maybe a year. We also believe that the weakest part of the operation was the 'drop'."

"What's that – the 'drop'?" asked the Secretary.

"That's the method of entry... how the operatives 'drop' the virus into the targeted system," the briefer replied.

"What does that mean?"

"Well, it means that the least sophisticated element is how they get into our systems, so the best line of defense is to never let it get into the system. We must deny access. The rapid growth in the use of flash drives is a huge threat. If someone takes work home on a flash drive, sticks it into their home computer – which is probably infected and then comes back into work and sticks the flash drive into a government computer—*BAM!* The entire system is infected. The worst thing for us is for someone to get access to any classified governmental programs, infect that system, and let it spread to the Anti-Missile Defense.

"Like, enter how? Where?"

"If a foreign operative could get into any of our systems—like NASA or the Space and Aeronautics computers, they would have easy access to everything."

"How could they do that?"

"Sir, their spies are everywhere. If they can ever get into our inner working systems, it's all over. Someone's giving us up for money."

"But don't we have safeguards for that sort of thing?"

"Yeah, but so did the Iranians."

"What do we consider to be our greatest threat?"

"Sir, our biggest threat would be a virus that disabled our Nuclear Missile Defense Systems. If we were hit by such a virus, it could severely impact our ability to deter a nuclear assault. We could eventually find it and fix it, but if an enemy were to coordinate their efforts, hit us with the virus and then, say within 48 hours launch multiple nuclear strikes, we'd be totally at their mercy. It could be a nuclear armageddon."

"Shit! And with Venezuela installing Iranian missiles within range of our cities, we're even more vulnerable."

"Yes, Sir," a staffer replied. "However, the greatest threat today is from China, especially their *Dong Feng* or "East Wind" and their *Juleng* or "Great Wave" systems. Both have ranges in excess of 8,000 kilometers and are capable of reaching the continental U.S. Both are MIRV capable."

Everyone around the table understood that he was referring to what is known in the trade as a Multiple Independently targetable Re-entry Vehicle. To the common man, that means the missile can carry a collection (multiple) of nuclear weapons, each capable of independently striking several targets or, if necessary, providing a redundancy in which several warheads strike the same target independently, all from one missile. One missile could strike six or eight cities along the Eastern Seaboard. One could take out all the ports in the Gulf of Mexico or one could hit New York City with as many as a dozen warheads. There would be nothing left but fire and ashes – all five boroughs and some parts of New Jersey – one missile!"

He continued. "Over the past decade, China has continued to strengthen its nuclear capability in all areas – size, range, accuracy, and most importantly, survivability. At present, we estimate that they have approximately 100 to maybe 150 nuclear weapons aimed at and targeted for U.S. cities. Multiply that by twelve warheads per missile and that's big trouble. If they could knock out our defenses, it would be brutal."

"What else could it do?" asked the Secretary.

"Well, another scenario would be to attack our power grids and/or communications. This thing is powerful. Knocking out a major power grid would be a disaster. For example, knock out the entire Northeast in the middle of winter – no lights, no electricity for heat, all traffic lights out of order, etc. It would be total chaos. They wouldn't have to hit us with missiles; in the chaos, we'd kill thousands of our own. Recent reports are that China has already operationalized a significant anti-ship ballistic missile system."

"I thought that was still a few years away," said the Secretary.

"Sir, I suggest you check with the Pentagon. They have more detail here. All I'm saying is that we have a bigger threat than we imagined."

"So, let me see if I understand what you're saying," cautioned the Secretary. "In the past, we've been desperately trying to stop spies from getting access to our secrets and intelligence, right?"

"Yes, Sir."

"But now," the Secretary continued, "our biggest threat could be for an enemy to insert a destructive device into our electronic communication and command and control system... in which case they no longer need to capture our secrets, they can act in a more offensive posture, while they have us on the ropes, so to speak?"

"Yes, Sir. That's it in a nutshell. And if we let them in, they'll be able to dictate our future. If they know – and we know—they could attack us without our having any capability to respond, well... we'd have to do whatever they told us to do. We'd be their slaves. No leader would risk millions of dead Americans – all in less than one hour's time."

The Secretary protested. "I don't believe China wants to destroy us. They'd have too much to lose, what with our owing them so much money and all. Why would they want to attack us? I've been to China. They're a friendly, likeable people."

"Well, Sir, our job is to consider probabilities. We're not in the business of possibilities or analyzing the mindset of other nations and their leaders. That's for you and the politicians to figure out; but when it comes to analyzing probabilities, that's our job. China is our number one threat. They have the greatest capacity of anyone to do us harm. Our job is not to read their minds as to what they want to do. Our job is to tell you what they're capable of doing and if we're to deny belief in their capabilities, that's like hiding our heads in the sand. If what we're looking at is true, it means that our fate and the fates of our children may no longer be in our hands, they may well be in the hands of the Chinese. We've been in denial so long that we refuse to face reality. Yes, China may never attack us; however, when the day comes that they no longer need us – what then?"

"And," added another, "in recent years, China has been growing its military faster than any other nation on earth... and the buildup has not all been defensive weapons. A lot of their new weapons are built on our technology. What we don't give them, they steal somehow."

The Secretary paused. He didn't like the briefer's tone of voice, but held his comments. "I need to talk to the President and the Joint Chiefs. Hold this information 'close hold' until I get back to you." The secretary rose and left the room, signaling to his aide.

"Yes, Sir?"

"Call my friend General Walls at the Pentagon. See if he's free for lunch."

"Yes, Sir."

The following day the Secretary and the General met for lunch.

"So, Tom," the Secretary began, "what do you make of all this cyber stuff – Stuxnet, Wikileaks, and such?"

"Well," the General replied, "I see an increasing sophistication almost daily. There was a time when cyber threats were considered bothersome hacking by a bunch of pimply-faced kids around the world. That's no longer true. Why do you ask?"

"My people are very concerned about the uptick in Chinese activity and I wanted your 'off the record' opinion."

"Well, we're in a much more sophisticated environment now and there's big money involved – both from criminals and from nation-state investments. Your guys have reason to worry."

"What or *who* do you consider to be our greatest threat?"

"Well, off the top I'd say the one with the greatest intent to do harm. Hell, every nation now has the capacity to do harm. The key is to establish priorities based on what we determine to be their intent."

"Okay, then what do we do about it?" asked the Secretary.

"The first thing is to recognize the changing nature of the beast. We have become accustomed to the idea that our network capabilities are merely conveniences that allow us to do more with less. We have to begin using these capabilities – and recognizing them as being fundamental and essential to all of our operations, especially our global security missions. It's a nasty world out there and we cannot remain free and on top if we neglect the facts of life."

Damn," the Secretary shook his head. "That's essentially what my staff told me yesterday. Thanks."

"Well, you've got a smart bunch over there, so listen to them."

"Thanks, I will."

"Another thing," the General continued. "There are a lot of 'Chicken Littles' running around out there. Don't fall in with them. We're really getting better at cyber security. We've busted several multi-million dollar espionage efforts in just the last two years. The key is for all of us to stay alert. Change our mindset on how to detect and then how to respond to cyber attacks; but we are getting better. The key is attribution. Once we find out who's trying to attack, we're damn good at the response."

J. Edgar Hoover Offices of the FBI

Across town, Charles Moonhaven, the Director of the FBI asked his assembled staff. "So, now what?"

"Well, Sir," the staffer began, "we have jihad cells popping up all over the country. They're using the Internet as their primary means of communicating. Their level of sophistication is growing so fast it's hard for us to keep up with them."

"What now?"

"Well, they've been flooding the Internet with websites and articles and blogs about the wonders of Islam. We think that they're hiding a lot of messages to jihadist organizations in these blogs and websites. The difficult part is their sophistication at encoding and the use of secret communication techniques. They even call it a science – 'concealment science.' Two aspects are especially disturbing: steganography and steganalysis. Steganography is the art of hiding messages inside ordinary text. Steganalysis is the flip side of it – the art of detecting hidden messages. With these two techniques they can hide data in innocuous-looking images. They use image pixels and mathematical equations to hide data. Their favorite software program is the "Secrets of the Mujahedeen" software application because it's a dual system that hides encrypted data in a picture and successfully combats steganalysis methods – and they're damn good at it. They can hide multiple messages in simple image pixels. Although we know there's a lot of chatter going on, it's difficult for us to break their codes and derive useful analysis."

"How is our Suspicious Activity Reporting doing?" The Director was referring to a national surveillance program called "SAR." Following 9/11, there had been numerous Islamic jihad threats to bring more and greater terror here to American soil. All federal agencies had cooperated in developing several anti-terror programs. Most had been abandoned due to the ACLU, which challenged nearly every program. Many were abandoned for lack of manpower, money, and other resources. However, many others had been working in concert with state and local agencies to improve our national security. The Suspicious Activity Reporting program had identified thousands of suspicious activities, but that resulted in only a few – less than fifteen arrests nationwide. The FBI had identified and neutralized the vast majority of threats, but the activity had drained much of the vitality of the Bureau.

The staffer shook his head. "Sir, Americans don't seem to care. They still don't believe it can happen here like it is happening in the rest of the world. About the only place where folks don't give us a hard time is right along the border with Mexico. Folks there know all about the Muslims being brought in by Mexican 'coyotes' who get paid big money for bringing illegals into America. The cartels know the best money to be had is from the jihad groups. Areas near the border are loaded with Muslim prayer blankets and stuff – even some Korans – that have been lost – or discarded by these radicals coming into the country. Some of them already know how to build bombs. The cartels get papers for them, everything they need to make them look legal. Once they're in our country they drop out of sight. It's hard to keep tabs on them."

Another staffer added, "Most Americans resent our surveillance efforts. They call it 'Big Brother.' Is that where the country is headed? Are we the enemy now?"

"What more do we have on the jihad websites?" asked the Director.

"Actually, we get less and less. Ever since the folks in the White House started prosecuting the CIA folks for 'aggressive interrogations' our intel has all but shut down. I'm not saying I blame the CIA. If I thought the White House gang was going to prosecute me for doing my job I'd do very little myself. The DOJ has now probably prosecuted more of our own agents than they have terrorists. Sometimes I think the DOJ is the center of our problem."

"Yeah, it's tough. Lots of my buddies have quit the CIA for that very reason."

"And that allows the terrorist groups to become bolder. They're openly calling for Sharia Law to be imposed on America and they respond to any comments about terrorism by calling law enforcement personnel 'terrorists.' They believe they are Holy Warriors and Mujahideen. More and more liberal judges are letting them get away with pushing Sharia Law on American citizens."

"Damn, we'd better wake up soon or we may all be bowing to Mecca by next Christmas."

"Or just not allowed to even mention Christmas without being sent to jail as some kind of hate monger," another staffer added.

Somewhere in the northern USA

The doors to the main training hall opened wide, allowing the assembled warriors to step into the early morning sun. They had just completed their morning prayers and were preparing for a day of intense training. Banners were hung from the surrounding trees, all proclaiming the call to "Kill the infidels, kuffars, and non-believers."

"Today," the Imam began, "your morning training will be to focus on building and detonating a bomb. However, it is important to remember that when you detonate your bomb it is not an isolated event. Timing and coordination are also important. When you begin your journey to heaven, do so in the company of your fellow martyrs. The days of the lone bomber are gone. Multiple bombs at different, but not too distant, locations will instill greater fear in the hearts of the infidels."

"Death to the infidels," the assembled warriors shouted. "Death to America!"

"The imam continued. "Your afternoon training will be on individual hand-to-hand combat, with emphasis on how to kill with only your hands – or any local materials that you may find in the area near you – a rope, a shovel, whatever. The most successful bomb attacks go unnoticed until the moment of detonation; however, on occasion, someone will be suspicious and may even try to stop you. You must know how to kill this person quickly so that you can complete your mission. The key point is to always be as the American Boy Scouts say, 'Be Prepared'." The Imam laughed at what he intended as a joke. The group did not understand and remained stoic.

"Remember, surprise is always your best weapon. The Americans are generally too busy to be aware of what is going on around them so stay in normal routines. Do not draw attention to yourselves until the time to act. It is also important to avoid trips outside of the U.S. If you establish a record of visiting Muslim countries, the FBI will watch you and they are very good. However, if you do not give them an opportunity to place their labels on you, then you can travel freely to the training sites here in America. And, when the time is right, you can join the martyrs of the past in heaven. Allah Akbar!" he shouted.

"Allah Akbar!" the recruits responded.

The new recruits went joyously to their instruction. They were preparing for an eternity as martyrs; however, they did not intend to die in vain. Each was committed to causing Americans as much death, pain, and suffering as possible. Their training was extensive. The instructors had all been in combat many times and had learned their lessons well.

Seven

"Once More, With Feeling"

"The continuing verbal battle between Senator Tibideaux of Louisiana and his defeated opponent is again in play," the newscaster said with a look of grave concern. "And it appears to have gone to a new level. Yesterday, the Senate Majority Leader issued a statement in support of Senator Tibideaux, criticizing his former opponent, John Bezzos, for his "vituperative comments" earlier this year. The Majority Leader suggested that Bezzos focus on his business and let Congress focus on the work of Congress. 'Let us also concern ourselves less with petty arguments and look at what Senator Tibideaux has accomplished for the great state of Louisiana,' the Leader had said. 'He has provided many jobs and other forms of relief for the people of his state.'"

The female co-anchor chimed in. "Yes, and then the battle heated up again when Bezzos responded with a statement of his own. 'Tibideaux cannot fight his own battles – he never could and since his wife remains in Louisiana, he needs someone else to fight his battles for him in Washington. I guess The Speaker has appointed himself the designated hitter. Tibideaux needs to 'man up.' Perhaps his wife could give him a lesson. I hear tell that she has all the gumption in the family. And as to the Speaker's suggestion that I let Congress focus on the business of Congress, I think that's a great idea – maybe one that Congress should honestly consider.

Does anyone out there believe Congress is doing anything to focus on the business of Congress – and our country? I'd be delighted to see Congressmen focus on the business of this country rather than their own self-promotion."

Johnny turned his face in the direction of Washington, D.C., cupped his hands to his mouth and yelled, "Hey, Congress! Are you listening? Get off your lazy ass and do your job!"

"Tell us what you think, viewers. Send us an email or click on our Facebook or Twitter links on our website," urged the male newscaster. "Should defeated politicians be allowed to belittle our elected officials? Is this a fair fight? We want to hear your comments about whether or not Congress is focused on the business of America."

Later, Melinda Bezzos met Johnny at the door. "I think you owe Mrs. Tibideaux an apology. I thought we agreed that families were off limits."

"You're right, Honey. I'll get on it."

"Damn right you will... tonight. In fact, do it right now. I know if Tibideaux had said anything about me, you'd be on him like flies on stinky stuff. No, you'd probably go find him and beat the hell out of him, so call her now."

Bezzos grinned, called the Tibideaux residence and apologized to Mrs. Tibideaux. "I spoke before I thought," he said. "Both my wife and I respect you greatly. It will not happen again. Although your husband and I have our disagreements, families do not belong in the spotlight. Again, I apologize."

"Why, thank you," Nicole responded. "Perhaps one day when all this settles down we can all have dinner together – maybe even be friends."

"That would be nice," Johnny replied. "Thanks."

"And tomorrow," Melinda added as Johnny hung up the phone, "I think you should also clarify – and apologize to your staff.

Wouldn't want them to think they needed to help you with self-mutilation – if you know what I mean. After all, you did violate your own rule."

"Yeah," Johnny agreed, understanding fully her reference to his speech to his staff about how someone would be treated if they violated the sanctity of the family.

First thing the next morning, he apologized to his staff for having violated his own rule about families. "This is why we all have to keep a sharp eye out for such a screw-up. What I did was wrong—and I only corrected it because my wife kicked my ass. I'm asking you guys to help me as well. And, I'll be watching you. We need to do this straight up."

Meanwhile, Nicole called Matthew and related the apology. Matthew's anger was attenuated a bit, but he was too busy to do anything more than acknowledge the apology. Matthew was still working at a frenzied pace. Later that week, he sent an aide to speak with the two newscasters. The aide was to also review and evaluate the emails, Twitters and Facebook comments. The station had broadcast the results the following day and the public generally favored the Senator over Bezzos; however, Matthew was interested in the tone and comments of the survey. He wanted to know more about the substance of the comments.

A couple of days later the aide returned and his report was largely favorable, as had been reported. By a ratio of about 5 to 4 the comments were supportive of Tibideaux and critical of Bezzos. The most common sentiment was that Bezzos should accept defeat gracefully and prepare better for any subsequent contests. Citizens also thought it was low of Bezzos to involve the Senator's wife. Most indicated that they were tired of the vicious word battles the politicians fought and wanted politicians to focus on the work of the government. Ten percent of the respondents believed the survey would not do any good. Their most frequent comment was, "Most politicians do not come to Washington corrupt, but nearly all become corrupt very soon thereafter... so your survey doesn't mean anything."

Tibideaux ignored the ten percent comments, but was pleased to know the voters preferred him over Bezzos. He thanked the aide and leaned back in his chair feeling greatly relieved.

"Excuse me, Senator," the aide spoke up as he reached the door. "There was one comment that came up twice and none of us knew what it meant. Perhaps it means something to you."

"Really, what was that?"

"Two comments came in, supposedly from someone who had been in the service with you. The comments were that 'Bezzos is right; Tibideaux is an R-E-M-F!'" The aide spelled out the letters. "Do you know what 'R-E-M-F' means?"

"What? Let me see that!" Tibideaux leaped out of his chair and came around the desk, snatching the report from the hands of his startled aide. His hands were shaking as he read the comments.

"God damn them! Who the hell do they think they are?" he screamed as his aide cowered against the door.

"Senator, what is it?" he asked.

"Nothing! Just get out! Get out now!"

The aide did as ordered. Tibideaux stormed around his office. "REMF! I'm not a goddamn REMF!" The veins in his neck looked like they were about to burst. His face turned bright red as rage surged through his body. "I am not a goddamn Rear Echelon Mother Fucker!"

For anyone who has ever been in a combat zone, it was the ultimate insult. Soldiers who do useful duty in rear areas are respected by combat soldiers. Front-line troops know they need support and rear area troops provide it. Every combat soldier knows that intelligence analysis, resupply, and the myriad of other details must be carried out if the guy with "boots on the ground" is to be successful—and as safe as possible. The combat soldier needs to be free to concentrate on the job at hand. He respects and appreciates support troops; but there are some in the rear areas merely to avoid the dangers of combat and they usually get these positions through politics or by ass-kissing superiors. These individuals are looked upon as scum by those providing real service – and by combat troops. They are known as REMFs: Rear Echelon Mother Fuckers. Not only are they reviled by combat and support troops, they are actually a drain on any unit, since the job they do is usually not one sanctioned by the Army, but created by local commanders – usually to make their own life easier—at the expense of the combat soldiers. Tibideaux could not sleep. He didn't like being called an REMF—even though he had truly been one. The term is derogatory enough and it's intensified by its very meaning, but for a combat soldier, it must also be uttered with the utmost contempt.

For the next two days Tibideaux wandered the streets of Washington, unshaven, unkempt, and ignoring his senatorial duties. He kept his coat collar turned up to hide or at least disguise his face. He even shut off his cell phone. His aides were frantic. Some called both his apartment phone and his cell phone every few minutes. They called his wife in Louisiana but she had no idea where he might be. Some camped out on his apartment steps; however Tibideaux managed to avoid them. He didn't want to talk to anyone. He needed to clear his head. *How can I get the respect I deserve? After all, I am a United States Senator – that has to count for something! I am **not** an REMF!*

As he ambled along a voice inside his head began to speak louder and louder. *Hey! Remember me? We are Colossus! Nobody fucks with us! They just don't understand! We must show them! You've got more guts than all of them combined!*

Yes, Matthew thought, *I am Colossus. I don't need to be wandering the streets – and I damn sure don't need to apologize to anybody. I am a U.S. Senator!*

With his head high and chin up, he turned to go home. The internal excitement was almost more than he could contain.

He returned to his apartment, cleaned up, got a good night's sleep, and then returned to the halls of Congress reinvigorated. For the next month he was a dynamo, working on projects, addressing constituents, making speeches. He appeared on national television in grand fashion. His voice was clear, his ideas sound, and his handshake firm. He procured additional funding for his client, Mr. Yao, as well as a few jobs for Louisiana. In exchange for favors to Yao, he received additional "packages." In exchange for the new jobs, he received the gratitude of the citizens of Louisiana.

"What have you been feeding the Senator?" a local politician asked Nicole Tibideaux.

"What do you mean?" she asked.

"Why, he's all over the place, stirring things up. He's more active now than he was during his campaign. Is he thinking of something bigger, politically?"

"Why no," she laughed. "You know how he is. When he gets an idea, he can be very committed and passionate. He's just doing his job." She was very proud of him, but she was curious about where he'd been those few days.

The lingering effects of the oil spill continued to bring hardship to the people of the Gulf area. Fishermen were limited to where they could fish. People around the country cut back on the amount of Gulf fish they would eat, worried about possible pollution. Oil field workers couldn't find jobs and the price of imported foreign oil continued to rise. All across America, citizens felt the pinch of the rising gas prices and with them other rising commodity costs. Wheat, corn, and sugar prices skyrocketed. Distribution of commodities requires transportation – and transportation costs are closely related to fuel costs. The luxury of an extra sandwich – at the current price for a loaf of bread, was no longer an option for an increasing number of Americans.

Matthew continued his fight for jobs. "We need to get the oil wells back into operation. It's critical for America – not just the Gulf coast. I intend to fight for those jobs," he said to the press. "I'm also working on bringing an additional 100 high level manufacturing positions to Louisiana. I know the task before me is daunting, but that's why the citizens of Louisiana sent me to Congress – to support the hard-working people of my state and I will do my job, come hell or high water."

"Well, Johnny," Melinda said at dinner, "looks like Tibideaux is building up his popularity with this effort for jobs."

"Yeah, I know," Johnny replied. "And the folks don't like me attacking him. Can't really say as I blame them. He sure is trying, but I just don't trust him. Do you think his wife appreciated my apology?"

"Yes, I believe she did. You were very sincere." She kissed his cheek. "You are ornery as hell sometimes, but you're not mean. Do you still want to run against him in the next election?"

"Well, guess we'll have to wait and see. Right now he'd be tough to beat, but you never know what tomorrow will bring. I still think I could do the country some good."

"I know you could. I just want you to be sure it's worth all the crap you'll have to go through, Honey." Melinda gently touched his arm. "Are you sure you want to be involved with all this political stuff? I think it's turning you into a bitter person, more than I've ever seen in you... and more than I want to see. You need to lighten up."

"Damn good question," he answered. "But it's tough. You see, I really think we need to change the way they do business in Washington. I think we need more Senators and Congressmen and women who are patriots first. We have too many self-serving assholes there. I'd hoped the Tea Party folks would change all that. Some of them have, but some just lost their values and fell into the 'business as usual' syndrome. Now, the more I get involved, I see how tough it is." Johnny glanced up at the ceiling. "You see, I realize now that everyone in this world has their price – *everyone*. That means I must have a price as well, I just don't know what that price is. Fact of the matter is that most people have no idea what their price is to go against all their deep-seated values.

"Our society has become so in love with money and stuff that we don't even think about it. Then we get an offer that we know is wrong but we rationalize that everyone else is doing it, so it's okay. I'd hate to get elected to office and find that my price is so low that the bastards could buy me. I think I could hold out and keep my principles and values, but I'm almost afraid to take the chance – you know, to even be put to the test. Honey, I'd rather die than ever find that there's a price at which I'd sell my soul."

Melinda grabbed his face with both hands. "Baby, look at me. I know you. There's no way on God's green earth that anyone could buy you. You're too strong and your values are too deep. Honestly, I don't think I want you to get elected to anything because I want you home, but I'm not worried about anybody ever buying you!" She kissed him hard on the lips.

"Thanks," he replied, "but you saw how I slipped up and involved Tibideaux's wife, even after I told the gang to leave family alone. See, to some degree, that was one of my prices – do whatever I need to do to win an argument. I was wrong."

"Yes, that was wrong... a mistake, but you corrected it immediately."

"Never should have happened. How many other folks have gone into politics who were clean, had the right values, and had always acted upon them, but then got elected and fell victim to the power their new position provided? Lots. Maybe that screw-up of mine was a sign and..." He paused. "You were the one who made me get off my ass and apologize. Don't know if I would have had the guts without you."

"Well, maybe it was a sign. Just don't let it happen again. I'm sure you won't, but if you do, I'll always be here for you. Actually, I'm not as worried about that as I am about you getting all heated up and flying off the handle without thinking it through. Remember what your dad sometimes says, 'Don't let your alligator mouth overload your hummingbird ass.' That's not just a funny saying. Your quick temper could cause you to take on a fight bigger than you can handle. Enough of this, I need you to help me with some chores, so get off your butt and come with me."

"I thought we got rid of all those 'honey-dos' last week," Johnny teased.

"Never happened," Melinda replied. "And probably never gonna happen. That's why I keep you around – to take care of my 'honey-dos'."

"*Oh my God!*" he moaned. I am had for life! Okay, let's do it."

In Washington, the pace was wearing Tibideaux down. He was feeling very, very tired and needed more energy, something like what he felt when Colossus was with him – when he was "the man!" He remembered the exhilaration and the sense of power of Colossus. Opening his closet, he removed the Remington and cradled it. Colossus smiled.

Tibideaux had followed a simple plan to avoid the possibility of detection for his first kill. He'd taken a cab to the airport, then the shuttle bus to a rental car agency where he'd rented a non-descript car. He'd then returned home and later conducted a recon of likely target areas. When he'd identified the area he wanted to target, he merely brought the rifle along. Thus, as he drove through the city, the chance of being recognized was greatly reduced. He liked the simplicity of the plan and followed it for this second venture. The only change was to use a different rental car company. Each time he splattered mud on the license plate to conceal the numbers.

A sudden early snow had fallen on the national's capitol city, creating slush at the edges of the street. The snow had lessened, but continued to fall lightly. For several hours he drove slowly around. Just after midnight he found himself on Suitland Road – not far from the scene of his first kill. He drove past many people on the streets – some alone and some in groups. Twice he stopped momentarily, considering possible targets, but something wasn't right so he drove on. There were no viable targets. "Damn!" he muttered, getting frustrated and discouraged. Turning onto a deserted street, he slowed the car. Through the windshield wiper blades he spotted a man lingering on a corner, wrapped in a heavy coat and wearing an old hunting hat with the ear-flaps pulled down over his ears. As Tibideaux drove past, the man shivered, hunched up his shoulders, and pulled his coat tighter.

Bingo! That's our target! Colossus whispered. Tibideaux grinned and nodded in agreement. He continued driving for another block, turned at the next corner, and then stopped. He knew what had been wrong with the other potential targets – it was not the targets, it was him! He was alone. He couldn't hear Colossus supporting him. Suddenly, Colossus was with him, helping him, assuring him of his courage. This was the right target. He cut the engine and stepped into the brisk night with his Remington cradled comfortably and at the ready. He moved methodically, with the stealth he had practiced as a boy hunting rabbits and with firmness like he'd seen Rambo do in so many war movies. With careful, measured steps, he put one foot in front of the other, never losing sight of his target. He was totally focused – the consummate hunter as he surveyed the street where the man was standing.

The man was still there, alone, leaning against a street light. He took a long, slow draw on his cigarette and then flicked the ashes onto the ground. He absent-mindedly glanced around, not in an effort to see anything, but merely an old habit.

Tibideaux scanned the area. Other than the target, the street was empty. He braced himself against the corner building and raised the rifle, holding it firmly. He took a long, slow, measured breath and then exhaled slightly as he steadied his aim. The man's chest was squarely in his sights. Slowly, he squeezed the trigger.

Whut! The man grabbed at his chest and staggered backwards. Matthew fired again, now at a moving target. *Whut!* The second round struck the man full in his chest, spinning him around. He took one more step and fell forward on his face.

Yeah! He was elated. He'd been accurate with his second round, even though the target was moving. *Damn! I'm even better than I thought!* Colossus was proud. They returned to the parked car and departed unseen.

The body was found early the next morning by a business owner opening his store. The same detectives investigated the shooting as had worked the first murder.

"Two identical shootings in the same general area, all within a few months. Gives me a bad feeling," said Ramon Gutierrez, the lead detective.

"Yeah. This guy has had some training. He knows what he's doing. But I can't make anything out of it. Why this guy? Why here? Why now? Any ideas?"

"No, but you're right. He's smarter than the average bear. In both cases either shot would have been a kill. He's organized and knows how to follow through on a mission. It appears he walked through the slush in the gutters. There's no footprints on the sidewalk anywhere. I don't think this snow is heavy enough to cover up tracks, but hell, two cars driving in the slush takes care of that. He plans well and cleans up after. Why? Are these random shootings or is there some connection? He obviously makes the kill from a distance so I doubt if there's anything personal here. He just has an urge to kill, but he doesn't stick around to gloat. He kills, cleans up, and leaves."

Sandra Rounds, his partner, had something to say. "It's different this time. He doesn't have to stick around to gloat because the news is on the TV, probably before he even gets home."

"You're right. I think we're going to see more of his handiwork before this is all over. We need to get the word out. Got any friends in that profiling bunch who could help us?"

"Yeah, I'll give 'em a call. See what I can find."

"Good. When you get the info together, let's do some brainstorming. There's gotta be something, we're just missing it. I don't want to end up with some crazy serial killer and get the city all shook up," said Ramon.

"Yeah, not to mention the Mayor all over our asses," Sandra replied.

The detectives spent several days reviewing security camera recordings. Some had been erased, some were not operating properly, and the few that had been operating provided limited information. They were able to identify a specific late model car in the area at the time of the shooting, but they were unable to get a clear picture of either the driver or the license plate, so they were no better off than they'd been the night of the shooting.

Back in his apartment, Tibideaux was pumped. He strutted around like a robot as adrenaline coursed through his veins. "I am Colossus! I right wrongs and punish the guilty," he boasted to himself while scanning the TV for any mention of the latest shooting.

"Good Morning, Washington!" the perky announcer smiled at the camera. "Well, there's been another murder near the Anacostia area." She lost the smile and affected a serious look. "The circumstances are similar to the shooting earlier this year. The police have issued a warning to homeless men in that area to try to find a shelter at night and to avoid being alone on the streets after midnight. Anyone having information on these shootings, please contact the Metro police."

"Yeah!" Tibideaux thumped his chest and shouted, "Hey, Bezzos. I got somethin' for your ass! Best you don't fuck with me!" As he danced around the room he was interrupted by Colossus, who restrained him.

Yes, we were good, but I want you to consider this. These were not worthy targets. We need to find targets worthy of us. We must right wrongs and punish the guilty! We must do more than merely remove a drain on society. We have a commitment to do more."

Tibideaux stopped strutting. "Yes," he agreed, drawing his body to a position of military attention. "We need to find targets that are not merely a drain on society, but harmful to society. Maybe I didn't kill any enemies in war, but I can help rid the city of scum."

Reinvigorated, Tibideaux again became a dynamo of activity. He had a mission. The Speaker's Transportation Appropriations bill was approved, not only thanks to Tibideaux's vote, but by his effective lobbying as well. The speaker was pleased and assured Tibideaux that he'd get a powerful voice in how the money was used in Louisiana. Tibideaux also led the Congressional effort to lift the ban on oil drilling in the Gulf of Mexico. The ban had greatly impacted the economy of Louisiana and was a major factor in the high unemployment rates in all of the Gulf States. Also, the loss of the Gulf oil had increased America's demand for Middle East oil – raising gas costs to exorbitant levels. Tibideaux's "out front" position on jobs made him extremely popular, not only in Louisiana, but in all of the Gulf States from Texas to Florida.

Along the Gulf Coast, many citizens sent faxes and emails—and made phone calls to their own elected officials. Some of the communications were fairly polite: "When are you going to join Senator Tibideaux in the fight for jobs? Others, however, were much more abrasive: "When are you assholes going to stop playing with each other and start taking care of the folks who elected you? Is Tibideaux the only politician who cares about us?"

The American public had held some hope of a change in Washington after the initial rise of the Tea Party. Now, however, since some of the new members of Congress had fallen into the trap of "the way business is done in Washington," the sense of disillusion was rampant throughout the nation. Tibideaux was becoming the shining star of Congress. He was also applauded by the press. They called him "The People's Senator." He was pumped and walked through the halls of Congress with a new swagger. He was invited to many gatherings where other Congressmen and Congresswomen could be seen with him and to bask in the glow of his successes. Pride pulsed through every fiber of his body. He contacted Yao for another package of dinner and an evening of pleasure. Yao was more than happy to comply.

Meanwhile, at the Department of Homeland Security there was a series of meetings and conferences. Experts were brought in from all branches of the government. Anyone with an interest in counter-intelligence, counter-terrorism, and cyber warfare were brought to the meetings. The results of these meetings were prepared in briefing form and given to select Congressional Committees by representatives from the Department of Homeland Security. Tibideaux was absent the day his committee was briefed because he was giving a speech in New Orleans on his next move to bring jobs to Louisiana. Upon his return to Washington, he was informed that the Department of Homeland Security had determined that spies from China were now a greater danger than those from Russia. All Congressmen and women were advised to be especially alert for security issues involving the Chinese. He called Fred Ming Yao for a meeting.

"Good morning, Senator." Fred was immaculately dressed, as usual. "To what do we owe the honor of this visit?"

The senator looked around the office for Sue Guifei. She was not there. "Oh," he said, "I just wanted to check with you on the status of our project. The paperwork for the contract appears to be moving well. Will you be ready to begin hiring once the contract is approved?"

"Most definitely. We are anxious to begin."

"Good. I also want to caution you that our Department of Homeland Security believes that Chinese spies and operatives are now more of a danger than the Russians. Did you know that?"

"Why, no! I do not keep up with such things as spies. I have a business to run. Why would my country need spies here in America? We are the greatest trading partners in the world. Our economies are strongly tied to each other. I do not understand."

"Neither do I," the Senator responded. "But it is important that whatever we do in our business, that everything is on the 'up and up'."

"What does that mean, 'up and up'?" Yao asked.

"Legal and honest, open..." Tibideaux replied.

"Yes, I see," Yao answered. "Most assuredly, business must be honest and open."

"Good. If you are approached by anyone, I trust you will advise me right away?"

"Yes, most assuredly."

"Have you been contacted by any Chinese Intelligence people?" asked the Senator.

"Why, no. Why would they contact me?"

"Well, you will have access to some pretty high level information. I just want to make sure that we are not involved with any spy activities."

"Certainly."

"Good. Well then, I believe we are through here. Please give Ms Guifei my regards."

"Yes, Senator. She will be sorry to have missed you. Please call if there is anything we can do."

Tibideaux left Yao's office with an extra spring in his step. *That's the way to maintain control. Establish the parameters up front and let them know who is boss.* He whistled an old Cajun tune as he returned to his office.

Later, Yao and Guifei met to discuss the meeting.

"Do you think he is suspicious?" Guifei asked.

"I do not think so," Yao replied, "but we must keep a close eye on him. We are too close to success in this operation to allow him to suddenly become patriotic. That would ruin everything. To our advantage, like so many American politicians, he has an overblown ego and sense of importance – in addition to being addicted to money and sex."

She interrupted. "But I thought there were others like us, working with other politicians. He is not our only contact, is he?"

"No, there are several other operations. It is vital that we attack them from many directions. This way, even if one attempt fails, there are others to carry on. But if we can be the ones who accomplish the mission, we will be national heroes. We must not fail."

"Is there anything more I can do?" she asked.

"Perhaps," Yao replied. "When he looks at you, the lust pours from his eyes like the sap from a young tree in springtime. Perhaps you should be personally involved in his next package," he smiled. "I think you would like that also, wouldn't you?"

Sue Guifei blushed. She had a job to do for her country and the Senator was, in fact, an enemy of her nation. *But there is no harm in having pleasure and being happy in your work. He is an attractive man.* Turning to face Yao, she replied, "I will do my duty for my country." Yao grinned at her reply.

Yao arranged a meeting with his intelligence handler. "The Americans are getting nervous," he reported.

"Yes, we know. It is vital to our national interests that you allay his suspicions. What are his weaknesses?"

"Sex and money."

"The usual, then?"

"Yes. He seems to have a special interest in agent Guifei. I will arrange for him to explore her offerings. That will keep him occupied – at least until we can get into their electronic infrastructure."

"How is that progressing?" asked the handler.

"Good. We expect the contract any day now."

"Good. Keep me informed. If I can be of service, do not hesitate to call. Remember, you are part of the vanguard to the new world order. When we are successful, China will be the single greatest power in the world. America will be our slave." They shook hands, bowed, and departed.

Eight

"A Chink in the Armor"

"Sir, you called for me?" Sam Spade addressed his boss, the Inspector General for the Louisiana Department of Transportation.

"Yes, Sam," his boss replied. "I have received some reports concerning possible irregularities with one of the state's contractors. Could you check it out for me?"

"Yes, Sir. I'll get right on it."

Sam collected all of the documents and went down the hall to his own office. He grabbed a cup of coffee, loosened his tie, and sat down. Opening the file, he began to carefully read each page, taking notes as he went along.

Sam was known as a meticulous investigator. He'd been with the department since his graduation from college, except for his two tours during the Second Gulf War. He still maintained his Active Air Force Reserve status and never missed a day of training, except when out of state on an investigation.

On the surface, the complaints and reports did not seem out of the ordinary – a failure to file required documents, contractor late on getting required clearances and so forth. Then he read one sentence that starkly stood out from other mundane comments. "In my opinion, Matthew Tibideaux is on the payroll of this Chinese company. He is illegally helping them to get contracts ahead of other, better qualified companies. He is a crook." Sam quickly looked to see if the letter had been signed. It had not.

Wow! Sam thought. *That's a pretty heavy-duty charge. I need to get to the bottom of this quickly.* Sam knew only one guy named Tibideaux powerful enough to have this kind of influence – Senator Tibideaux... *and the Senator's first name is Matthew.* Sam ran his fingers through this thick head of graying hair. He was fully aware of the dangers of making rash charges against someone with the power of a U.S. senator. It would be a touchy investigation. He called his boss and relayed the information he had uncovered.

"So you think it could be the Senator?" asked the Inspector General.

"God, I hope not, but we do need to investigate."

"Yes," his boss agreed, "but *very* carefully. What assistance will you need?"

"For now, I just need some time. I'll wrap this up as soon as possible and report back. Again, hopefully it's just some disgruntled person and no real problem. I'll be discreet."

"Good. Keep me posted."

Sam spent the next three days reviewing documents, including bids and awards given to various contractors. He followed all possible leads relating to possible "peddling of influence" and other offenses. On his white wallboard he built a flow-chart diagram, identifying all possible linkages. The papers on his desk were sorted by category and stacked neatly. Comments about the U.S. Senate sub-committee on transportation did appear in connection with one Chinese owned company, Future Technology, on more than one occasion. Sam "googled" the sub-committee; Matthew Tibideaux was a prominent member. Sam paid a visit to the Louisiana office and factory of Future Technology, Inc., a company owned by Fred Ming Yao. The manager was helpful, but appeared to know very little. He ran this local operation, building and modifying microchips according to the production design orders he received from the main office, which was in Washington, D.C. He did not even know what the final purpose and usage was to be for these chips. He merely followed the production design. Recognizing a dead-end, Sam booked a flight to the nation's capitol.

Two days later, Sam entered the headquarters of Future Technology, Inc. and was escorted to the office of the Executive Vice President for Operations, a Ms. Sue Yang Guifei, an attractive lady in her early to mid-thirties who obviously respected her own body. She was very pleasant and offered to allow Sam to examine any and all company documents.

Sam met with her for about two hours. She appeared very open and cordial, but in his years of experience as an investigator, he had developed an ability to see behind the facades people presented and he had an uneasy feeling about this woman.

That night as Sam sat in his hotel room reviewing his notes, there was a knock on his door. "Yes, who is it?" he asked.

"I need to speak with you," a voice answered.

Sam cautiously opened the door, leaving the emergency locking hook in place. In the hallway stood a man in his mid-fifties, wearing a nice suit, with matching tie.

"Yeah?" Sam asked.

"I have information on Future Technology and Senator Tibideaux," he whispered.

Sam opened the door and invited him in, motioning to the easy chair in the corner.

As the man entered, Sam subconsciously moved his arm slowly backward until the heel of his hand rested on the butt of his .357 SIG.

"You the one who wrote the letter?" he asked.

"Yes, and I believe it's even worse than I had indicated."

"So, what's your name? Why did you write the letter?"

"Are we safe here?" the man asked.

"Far as I know."

"Okay, I'm Joe Scorso." He held out his hand. "I've been working for Future Technology for about two years and I've seen some shady stuff."

"Sam Spade." Sam took the man's hand and shook it firmly. "So talk to me," he said.

"Okay, here goes."

Joe launched into a number of stories and incidents that Sam would have found hard to believe if he hadn't been in the business for so long. Joe was very thorough, mentioning names and dates. "This guy Yao is some kinda big shot back in China and he's getting rich stealing secrets and stuff from us. It's nothing big, but I've seen classified documents that are here one minute and gone the next. I've been careful not to ask questions, not just to keep my job but because I'm scared. If they really are spies and find out I turned them in, I'm dead. I've got a family. I figured it was my duty to say something, but this puts me between a rock and a hard place. Reporting crap against a powerful politician—hell, with our system – he's the crook and yet I could be the one to wind up in jail. On the other hand, piss off this Chinese guy and hell, I could wind up dead. Ya know what I'm sayin'?"

"Yeah, you did the right thing," Sam assured him. "But why?"

"Well," said Joe, shaking his head slowly, "my Dad was a veteran. He used to tell me that a veteran is someone who, at one point, wrote a blank check made payable to 'The United States of America' for an amount of up to and including their life. That's honor and there are way too many people in this country who no longer understand it. My dad spent two years as a Casualty Assistance Officer, you know, those guys who have to go tell families that their sons and daughters have 'bought the farm' – you know – that they've been killed in the line of duty to our country. He had to retire after those two years. Ripped his heart out every time he knocked on a door or presented that folded flag to a grieving parent or spouse or small child who no longer had a daddy. 'Til the day he died, he could still hear some of those folks screaming 'No! No! Not my child!' Then to see what a sleazy bastard this senator is, willing to sell out his own country for a few lousy bucks – he's a scumbag! I've overheard both Yao and his partner, Sue Guifei, talk about how they own him and that he takes orders from them. Now if that ain't wrongheaded, I don't know what is."

"What do you mean, 'they own him'?"

"I don't know, but I guess they've bought him off. I'm sure he's on the take. He uses his position to get them contracts. I don't know what contracts they got for Louisiana, but they do seem to work hard to get into NASA and the FAA. They are very interested in space, aviation, and space communications. Oh yeah, and once I saw one of Yao's buddies personally place some specialized electronics components in a box and send them to China. Later, I saw the customs form and what he listed was microchips or something. That seemed suspicious to me."

"And you think the Senator is aware that he is jeopardizing the nation's security?" Sam asked.

"What the hell else could it be?" Joe asked in return. "I don't buy this crap that he's just working for his constituents. That doesn't work for me. And even if it did, once you become a crook that negates anything good you might have done – at least in my book."

Sam listened for nearly two hours, recording everything that was said and occasionally making notes. "Okay," he said, as they wrapped up the conversation, "let me process this. I'm probably going to need more information. Are you willing to try and gather more? I don't want you to take any unnecessary chances, just keep your eyes and ears open and let me know, okay?"

"Sure."

Sam instructed Joe on how to reach him and assured him, "Your communications will go directly to me and no one else."

It was nearly midnight when Joe left. "Thanks," said Joe. "We gotta stop this stuff."

Sam spent an additional two days in Washington, contacting old friends who might be able to help him gather additional information on Future Technology Inc and its two principals Fred Ming Yao and Sue Guifei. He knew that he had to be cautious asking about a U.S. senator, but he did find an Air Force buddy who was a semi-retired private investigator – "Spud" Wilkins. He'd gotten his nickname while in the Air Force because his shaven head looked like an Idaho potato. The additional weight he had gained since leaving the military only added to this image. However, folks who knew him knew he was an efficient and tenacious investigator. Sam filled him in without mentioning any names and asked Spud if he'd be willing to do a little pro bono work.

"Spud" was a true patriot. He'd served his time in Iraq, even though he was personally convinced that it was a bad war and that we shouldn't have been there, but then a lot of the guys serving had felt that way. They disagreed with the policy, but their elected officials had sent them. Most guys felt they had to believe someone in the government knew what they were doing. Later, most realized that they'd been lied to by the government, just as their fathers and uncles had been lied to during Vietnam.

"Look," Spud said, "I took an oath to support my country. I'm not sure I agree with what we are doing, but I gotta trust that my government does. Of course, there are times when I think this way.

I still want to support my country. That has never changed. What has changed is my trust in my government officials. I think C.S. Lewis said it best. I don't remember the exact words, but something like 'it is easier to suffer under really crooked types, because sometimes the crooks might let up.' The worst kind is the bunch who thinks what they are doing is the right thing because they never let up – always thinking what they're doing is good, despite evidence to the contrary."

Spud also made a silent pilgrimage to Arlington Cemetery every Veteran's Day. "These guys gave it all," he'd say, "so the least I can do is to show them some respect." Sam respected this man.

"Hell, yes. If there's a chance some politician is helping give away our secrets, I'd be happy to help catch the bastard. Is he one of yours?" "Spud" had already figured that it had to be a politician from Louisiana or why else would Sam be interested?

"Yes, It's a senator – Matthew Tibideaux."

"I'll be damned." Spud" shook his head, partly in disbelief and partly in disgust. "A senator?"

"Yeah."

"*Non-illegitimas carborundum!*" They both laughed at this reference to an old military saying: "Don't let the bastards grind you down."

"Yeah," Sam added. "It's tough enough to fight when your back is covered, but when your own leaders are lettin' 'em in through the back door, it's damn near impossible."

Sam returned to Baton Rouge the following day and reported to his boss. The Inspector General was greatly intrigued. "So, what's your take on this?" he asked. "Is there any sign of wrongdoing within or against the state of Louisiana?"

"Hard to say with what I've got, but it's damn sure wrongdoing against the country," Sam replied.

"Then technically it's not our problem, it's something we should forward on to the FBI... or maybe the CIA?"

"Yes, sir, probably so; but I'd like permission to stay on this for a few more days. By then we should know if we really do have enough to forward a full report or if we should just send a memo. If it's okay with you, I'd like to clean it all up a bit. I wouldn't want to see someone in D.C. go crazy and start a witch-hunt against the state of Louisiana for forwarding unwarranted accusations against a senator. We need to have all our facts together, wrapped up in one tight little bag before we notify the feds."

The Inspector General stroked his chin. "Hmm," he muttered. He had great respect for Sam. Although what Sam had asked for was somewhat irregular, the boss trusted his judgment. He also agreed that there was no need to take a chance on bringing grief to Louisiana over an incomplete report. "Okay, two weeks – win, lose, or draw."

"Thanks, boss." Sam hurried off to review the information he had.

He had been reviewing documents for about two days when he received a call from his friend in Washington. "Spud" was what lots of folks refer to as "an old war horse." He did most of his investigative work like an old-fashioned gum-shoe, but he did know how to use technology on occasion.

"Hey, buddy," Spud began. "Looks like you've got a real wing-dinger on your hands. I made some contacts with several friends and called in some old favors from the past and this looks like it could be espionage – maybe even treason. And it looks like there might be some high-level folks involved. You better watch your back. Is your boss in the loop on this?"

"Yeah," Sam assured him.

"This guy Yao is definitely a foreign agent," Spud continued. "He has had a guy working for him that should have disqualified him from government contracts. This employee at Future Technology, Inc. had previously pleaded guilty to falsifying customs information on shipments to China when he was working with another computer company. The trial was a murky one. The employee had been fined one thousand dollars and given a three-year probationary sentence in federal court. The shipments allegedly contained information involving classified space communications programs, but was never proven, since China would not return the packages. So they didn't slam him on espionage, but on customs violations. Then Yao hired this guy. By the way, this guy's lawyer is a good friend of your senator. All sounds kinda shaky. Your boy, Yao, spends a lot of time in China. And, in my opinion, your senator's brains appear to be in his groin. Rumor has it that he spends a lot of time with the ladies of the night – at the high-end. You gonna turn this over to the FBI?"

"Think they'd do anything?"

"Not the FBI that I'm concerned about. They'll give it a good shot, but then you gotta face the Congress and then the courts. That's when it all falls apart. Can you picture it? First, the Congress ethics folks will fuck around and render the evidence unusable because they definitely take care of their own. Look how many crooks we have in Congress. They get away with shit that would land you, me, or any ordinary citizen in jail. The Justice Department will go after us and then some liberal judge will throw out the charges against the senator and go after us for harassing a public figure or some such shit. How do you fight it?"

"Yeah," Sam agreed. "We have to make this case air-tight before we say anything."

"Makes me wonder about the theory of the *Shadow Government* – you know that book?"

"No, I don't."

"Well, the theory is that a handful of radicals actually own the government and the top players. They want to build a one-world system where America becomes just another third world country. Our politicians don't have the power to stop it – or they just don't understand it so they ride along, kiss ass, and line their own pockets."

"Wow! That's some heavy shit! Where'd you hear this?"

"It's all over, but mostly folks are forced to keep it quiet."

"Well, that's too big for me right now. I gotta stay focused on the problem I have."

"I'll keep my eyes and ears open and let you know if I get anything. In the meantime, watch your back," Spud advised.

"Yeah, thanks for what you did. You're right. I'll send this through channels over to the FBI. That's what my boss thinks too."

Shortly after he'd finished talking with Spud, Sam's phone rang.

"Sam?" the voice whispered.

"Yes, who's this?"

"Joe Scorso," he whispered. "I think the Chinese suspect me of snoopin' around. Be careful. I'm gonna lay low for awhile."

Click. Joe hung up before Sam could reply.

Nine

"Colossus in Command"

"Good afternoon, Senator." Mr. Yao rose from the table and bowed slightly.

"Good afternoon, sir," the Senator replied, offering his hand. "What is the purpose of today's meeting?"

"Once our latest contract is finally approved, I would like to open another factory in Louisiana. It would offer between 50 and 100 new jobs, all skilled workers with above-average salaries. Would you like to help me?"

Tibideaux grinned. The nation was still suffering from high unemployment. Fifty to a hundred new jobs at the upper end would be a great strategic win for Louisiana and for him. "Absolutely," he replied. "And what else?"

It was Yao's turn to grin. *Fool*, he thought, but he said, "There will be a nice package and on this occasion, I may be out of town on business. If so, Ms. Guifei has volunteered to personally present the package – if that meets with your approval."

At the mention of her name, Tibideaux felt a tingle in his groin. "Package" was their code word for money and women. He felt no guilt. He was bringing jobs to his state and that was why the people elected him. He was doing his job – what the people of Louisiana wanted. He was a servant of the people and he was damn good at it! If he had to hold up both ends of a deal—that was okay. After all, it was his job and he was doing good things for his constituents. He rationalized to himself, *Sometimes the ends justifies the means...* and recalling his memories of her svelte body, he thought, *She is one fine 'package'!* His job just kept getting better and better.

"Yes, that will be fine," he replied, trying to appear unexcited.

He returned to his office and began working on several briefs in preparation for his next committee meeting. He was interrupted when Colossus paid him a visit. *Why are you sitting here?* Colossus asked. *You have done enough for Louisiana this week. You will provide jobs, but you have done nothing to help clean up the nation's capitol as you promised. Right wrongs and punish the guilty. You have an obligation!* Matthew tried to ignore Colossus because he had a lot of paperwork to complete and meetings to attend – all business for his constituents. He did not want to go out into the night. *Not now,* he insisted. *I really have to get all this work done before I have to brief the committee.* But Colossus was insistent. *Right wrongs and punish the guilty! Prove that you can strike against worthy targets!*

Reluctantly, Matthew agreed that Colossus was right. He returned to his apartment and tuned the TV to the local news channel. The station was doing a documentary on the rise of gangs in the metropolitan area. The list of crimes committed was extensive: murders, assaults, child prostitution, drugs. The reporter identified several gangs, but the one that caught Tibideaux's attention was the Mara Salvatrucha, better known as MS-13. The reporter described it as the toughest gang in the Washington, DC area – maybe even in the nation.

Matthew "googled" MS-13 and was amazed at what he found. Originally formed in El Salvador during a civil war, they were originally trying to help the poor to survive. Then, like so many organizations, they saw the opportunity for power and money, so they became corrupt and violent. Moving to Los Angeles, the gang took their name from two streets where they had been located: La Mara, a street in El Salvador and 13th Street in Los Angeles. They are reputed to be the most violent gang in America. They are highly organized, with factions in virtually every major city in the United States, as well as most of South America.

Interestingly, they are also one of the most prolific transporters of human trafficking in America. They are reported to be very active in bringing jihadist terrorists into the United States. Member's bodies are abundantly tattooed with hard graphics and the number 13. Recently, to confuse the police they have begun to use other numbers; however, when added together the numbers used always equal 13 – for example, "67" or "49."

Almost everyone has a nickname. The wilder and more dangerous you are, the more significant the nickname. Initiations are brutal, usually requiring the prospective member to perform a vicious criminal act, even the gang women. Having sex with all of the male gang members in a single night is not enough, the girls must also do something brutal. A random killing is the most common. Once a gang member, the only way to leave the gang is by death.

The more he researched MS-13, the more dominant Colossus became. *This is what we want – worthy targets. These people are scum. They can be called combatants in the war on terror. If they are helping bring terrorists into our country, then they are enemy combatants. We can conduct combat operations against them. We will be a warrior! They deserve to be punished. And, these dudes are tough. If you cap a couple of them, then you really are "the man." They cannot be allowed to come into this country and make a shambles of our laws and traditions. It is your duty to punish them!*

Matthew agreed and searched for additional information. The U.S. Border Patrol identified the Tucson sector of the border as practically overrun and under the control of Mara Salvatrucha. MS-

13 now appears to be in control of the flow of drugs, weapons, and illegal aliens into the U.S. Mara Salvatrucha has attracted the attention of al Qaeda and has formed an agreement to smuggle terrorists and weapons into the United States. Al Qaeda pays them well. MS-13 does more than smuggle them across the border, they also provide the terrorists with counterfeit "matricula consulars." These cards verify that the bearers are Mexican citizens who are living outside of Mexico with the government's permission. This allows the terrorists to move around inside the U.S. and elude the governmental "watch lists." As these illegal aliens enter the U.S. their travel routes have become littered with jihadist propaganda discarded along the way.

See? Colossus spoke loudly. *I knew we could find worthy targets. Taking them out would be even better than a combat mission in Iraq. Here they are on U.S. soil! This is what you need! You are the nation's defender!*

The MS-13 faction in D.C. controlled an area known as "The International Corridor" stretching from Langley Park, Maryland to the Tokoma/Langley crossroads in Washington. Matthew "googled" Mapquest and the satellite images of the area. He compared this information to a street map of the area and then he drew his own map and patrolled the area. He mapped it out like soldiers do when on patrol in enemy territory. Soon he had every building, by address and name, and every side street committed to memory. He drove through the area many times—but at intervals and at different times of day. He also adjusted his clothing to disguise his appearance. Each visit he drove a different rental car, so as to minimize detection. Once he even took the bus. He wasn't satisfied until he knew the area by heart. *Reconnaissance and deception*, he thought. *Yeah, I shoulda been in Special Ops. I'm that good.* Colossus grinned. He respected the planning almost as much as he respected the action. Matthew was becoming a good student and Colossus was pleased.

Matthew drove carefully to The International Corridor. At approximately 2:00 a.m. he drove past a group of five young men and two women gathered on a street corner. Openly drinking and smoking, they were loud and boisterous.

The bastards, Colossus whispered. *These guys are what we're after. Together, who knows how many decent people they've robbed, or raped, or even killed and then were never required to pay for their crimes. Criminals must pay for their crimes. And if they are connected to terrorists, the punishment we render will be even more deserved. These are the guys we want. It is time to punish them. At least one of them will never bother decent citizens again – not after tonight! You and I will administer their punishment. It's the right thing to do.*

Tibideaux nodded his agreement and then drove one block past the group and turned into a side street. There were no other people on the streets as he moved silently back to the corner, dropped to a prone position, and crawled slowly to the corner of the building. As he crawled, he cradled his rifle – the same way he had seen soldiers do in war movies. His silhouette was negligible in the subdued light. The group continued their loud and boisterous conversation unaware of their stalker. Matthew watched them for a few seconds and then drew one of the individuals in his sights. He began to draw a slow breath, but was interrupted by Colossus.

Wait! You are good enough for one shot, one kill. Why waste the second bullet? If you were in combat, wouldn't you try to kill as many as possible? You are good enough to take out two of them and still get away. Make this a really big night!

Tibideaux smiled and readjusted his plan. One member of the group was sitting against the light post. It would take him longer to move. Tibideaux mentally marked him to be target number two. For his first target he chose what appeared to be the leader – at least he was the most vocal and animated. Quickly checking the area, Tibideaux was satisfied that there were no other individuals in sight. Carefully bringing the leader into his sights, he fired the first round.

Whut! It caught the target in mid-sentence, interrupting his loud comments. He coughed, grabbed his chest, and dropped to the ground. The group heard nothing but his cough and momentarily they appeared confused, wondering what had just happened.

Whut! the man sitting against the pole jerked and then slumped. The entire action from the first round fired until the second man fell had taken less than five seconds. Tibideaux knew instantly that both would be dead before he reached his car. When the second man fell, the group scattered, pulling their own weapons as they looked for cover and for any signs of the shooter. A couple of them fired towards the corner Tibideaux had vacated only seconds earlier. Tibideaux quickly policed his expended ammo and ran to his car. The kill had been at slightly over one block away. He knew they could neither catch him nor identify him. *Hoooah!!* Colossus shouted in his brain as he drove away. *We punish the guilty!*

The adrenaline rush was the greatest he'd ever felt. *I did it all!* he thought. *Planning, preparation, stealth, deception! Efficient and cool under fire! Two shots, two kills. I am the man! I coulda been Special Ops! No, not coulda – I SHOULDA been Special Ops!* He returned to his apartment, showered, and went to bed.

During his breakfast the following morning, he tuned in to the local news channel.

"Good morning, Washington," the announcer began. "We have another random shooting in the nation's capitol. Police are trying to determine if this is a gang shooting or another random killing. They are saying only that the shootings are being investigated. Meanwhile, members of the gang are vowing revenge."

Tibideaux laughed as he prepared to go to work. He had an important day ahead of him. After all, he was a representative of the people and had other, equally important duties. As he entered the Senate, two separate meetings were being held in different parts of the city.

In the heart of the city, a team of detectives was being formed to look into the recent shootings.

"So what do we have? Do we think this is a serial killer?" one asked.

"Probably," Ramon Gutierrez, the new team leader replied. "In this latest shooting, the rounds were identical to those of the two homeless guys, but the M.O. is different. He only used one round per kill this time, but he doubled down on the number of victims. I think he must be gaining confidence to step it up this way, but we still have no idea why."

"Yeah," Sandra Rounds answered. "Maybe he just has one helluva death wish. Killing homeless guys is one thing. Bringing heat down on MS-13 is crazy."

"He better hope we get to him before they do."

"Yeah, but if they could get there first, it would save us a lot of effort – and money."

"Do you think this could be some kind of gang-related action and the homeless guys were just a feint, to throw us and MS-13 off-guard?" asked one of the detectives.

"Don't think so," Rounds answered. "I believe this guy is a crazy. Probably some frustrated guy who's been hassled at work and wants to prove himself. Whatever, we need to resolve this – and fast. We need to go back over all three crime scenes. The last thing we want to do is to cause a panic in the city – and one more shooting could trigger it."

In the International Corridor, MS-13 also held a meeting. Although not as sophisticated as the police meeting, it got right to the point.

"We gonna find this motherfucker and burn him bad."

Everyone nodded in agreement.

Ten

"Somewhere Near the Mexico-Arizona Border"

"Listen up. I am Juan." The man spoke with a commanding voice, in Spanish. "These are my men." He waved towards four armed men standing behind him. "We will be your escorts into the U.S. It will be a difficult trip and it could be very dangerous. You must do exactly as I say at all times. Is that clear?" Those in the group who spoke Spanish nodded in agreement.

One man turned to his partner and asked, "What did he say?" His partner translated, in Arabic.

The travelers were a mixed lot, numbering nine in total. Some were Mexicans seeking work on America's farms. One couple was from Venezuela. The young wife was pregnant and they were hoping to have the child born in America so it would have a chance for a better life. Two were merely human "mules" carrying a small fortune in cocaine from Colombia, destined for their brothers and sisters of the MS-13 gang in Washington. Two were radical Muslims on their way to join "sleeper cells" of terrorists waiting for an opportunity to strike against the "infidels" in America. All in all, they were not too different from the hundreds of groups crossing the border each week.

Juan, and his team of escorts did not care about their reasons for traveling; they were in it merely for the money. They were members of the notorious "Los Zetas," the most feared of all Mexican criminal bands. The "Zetas" had been formed by the various drug cartels for the express purpose of conducting smuggling missions from Mexico into the U.S. Eventually, they had become powerful enough to work for themselves and, of course, the highest bidders. They provided passage for smuggling of any kind: drugs, sex-slaves, terrorists, and the common people just wanting a job opportunity.

"Los Zetas" were known to be both fearless and ruthless. Most were originally members of elite Mexican Army units, men accustomed to hardships and heavy duty. They had been highly trained and equipped by American Special Forces. But military pay is meager in most armies and Mexico is no exception. They were lured into the smuggling business by the promise of significantly more money than the military could pay – enough to take care of their families in a style they'd never dreamed possible.

The choice for many had been a simple one. Upon joining, they were then taken to special training camps, where they underwent nine weeks of specialized additional training. The curriculum is extensive: Land navigation, the use of night scopes, radio and electronic communication, small unit combat tactics, and an understanding of how the American Border Patrol operates. Juan was typical of the leadership at the tactical level. He was a family man and wanted more for his family. Although he did not really like his job, the money was significantly better than Army pay and so he was efficient. He also knew that failure to perform could mean harm to his own family. Over time he had lost any sense of compassion.

The following morning, the travelers were rousted early, fed a sparse meal of goat meat and rice in tortillas, and then formed up for the trip. Each was given a canteen with water, a small bag of dried foods, and two cans of soup.

"Be careful," Juan advised them. "Do not waste any of your food and water. Resupply points are established along the way, but there is no guarantee they will always be there. When you are hungry and thirsty, it is a difficult trip. If you fall out, we will not stop to wait for you. You must stay with the group. Is that clear?" A nodding of heads. "Then, it is time to go," Juan ordered.

There were five members in the team. One was up front as the point man. He knew these routes well and was armed with a 12-gauge riot shotgun. On each flank one Zeta, armed with an AK 47, stayed a short distance away from the travelers. To the rear of the formation, the "tail-gunner" carried an M-60 machine-gun. Juan was the lead man on the right flank. Zakir Abdul, one of the Muslims, was impressed by the military precision of the Zetas and when they stopped for lunch, he approached Juan.

On a hunch, he spoke in English. "Your team is very professional. You have trained well. I congratulate you."

Juan was taken aback briefly and then replied. "Yes, we must be good. For us, failure is not an option. We must be better than the Federales, the American Border Patrol, and the banditos who would love to steal from us and so we must be well-armed and professional in their use."

The travelers were given only infrequent rest stops and marched all day across the desolate Sonoran Desert. The pregnant woman had difficulty keeping up and was constantly falling behind.

"Here, let us help you," a few of the travelers offered and took much of the load from her backpack.

"*Gracias, gracias,*" both she and her husband replied. Neither the Muslims nor the human "mules" offered assistance.

Like the rest of the travelers, her clothes were soaked from perspiration. Juan and the Zetas did not hesitate, nor did they offer any assistance. They maintained the pace, stopping only at an occasional *tinaja* to refill the canteens. Tinajas are natural rock basins found throughout the Sonoran that catch and hold rainwater. Although not clean, the water will quench one's thirst and serves as an occasional stopping point for the wildlife in the area.

After a short break for supper, they continued moving towards the border. At one point they climbed through a large hole in a fence that appeared to extend to the end of sight in both directions. It was in disrepair and most assumed it was the border fence, but none of the travelers knew for certain when they actually passed into America. It all seemed to be the same barren desert on both sides of the border. A flurry of bats passed over their heads as they crossed the fence and a pair of coyotes hunting pocket mice and kangaroo rats stopped momentarily to warily watch this parade of humans. The only noises the travelers could hear was the sound of their shoes scuffing the desert floor.

It was nearly midnight when Juan ordered them to halt and to get down. Abdul inched as close as he dared, listening to Juan on a phone.

"Yes, and both of you feel it is clear to move?" Juan listened for a second more. "Roger," he replied. His two border scouts had been in position for several hours now and had not seen any suspicious movement. Juan gathered the group. "We are only a few miles from a road. The road will take us to a major U.S. highway. We are in an area of land where the U. S. government will not allow the border patrol to operate. I do not know why, so do not ask. There are no other roads to that highway, only the trails and ravines like we have been traveling. As we get closer to the road, a paved road, I have a pickup truck and a driver who knows the trails. He will take us to this road and then to a major U.S. highway. Once on the highway, we will take you to Phoenix and then you are on your own. Stay with the group. If you fall back now, you are on your own. We will not stop for anyone. Time is critical – and be very quiet." Juan waved to his point man to move towards the meeting place. All were excited at the prospect of riding. It had been a long hard walk.

"C'mon, Sweetheart." The young husband coaxed his wife along, half carrying her while half-dragging his own feet forward. "We are almost there... just a little bit further." She gasped for air and moaned with pain.

"Okay, okay," she gasped.

They had travelled a little over a mile when suddenly they saw the bouncing headlights of the truck. It was perhaps only a half mile away, but they all could see it. Excitement rippled through the travelers and Abdul laughed softly.

"See, my love," the young man encouraged his wife. "Soon."

Then, just as suddenly a searchlight beam swept past them and returned, highlighting the group.

"Stop where you are," a voice announced through a loudspeaker. "U.S. Border Patrol."

The point man dropped to a prone position and fired in the direction of the voice and light. The Zetas on the flanks spread out and with their AKs on full automatic, also sprayed in the direction of the voice. The tail gunner dropped to one knee and surveyed the back trail, keeping his M-60 at the ready. It was his job to make sure they were not being surrounded. The truck had stopped and turned off the lights and both of the occupants had also begun firing in the direction of the light. The travelers had all dropped to the ground with the first sound of gunfire. They were frantically digging at the ground, trying to get lower and lower as the bullets flew all around them. All of the women were crying. Juan cursed.

Abdul was analyzing the situation. He scanned the horizon, both to watch the nature of the battle and to determine a course of action if the Border Agents should win. "By Allah," he whispered. "I should have a weapon. I could help these men."

One of Juan's men went down. Juan cursed again and ordered everyone to move on the Border Agents. The fight lasted less than ten minutes until both agents were dead. They had simply been outgunned.

"*Puta! El Stupido!*" Juan cursed and kicked the two dead agents, while also ordering the truck forward and the travelers up and moving. He didn't know if the border agents had alerted anyone else, but he wasn't about to give them any further opportunities. He fired one round into the forehead of each agent.

The truck stopped about 500 yards from the travelers and turned around. It was as far down the ravine as the truck could go. The travelers were all running fearfully towards the pickup; all, that is, except the pregnant wife. She could not get off the ground. Her husband had run about ten yards when he realized that she had fallen behind. He rushed back to help her. He called for help from the others, but no one responded; they continued running for the truck. The Zetas all moved towards the truck, crouching like large cats on a hunt. They were not to be caught off-guard again. They had little regard for the travelers. Each person had been ordered to board the truck. It was each individual's responsibility to do so.

Juan retrieved the weapon and wallet from his dead team member and jumped into the truck. "*Vamanos! Vamanos!*" he ordered.

"Wait, please wait!" the husband pleaded while trying to help his wife get to the pickup.

"*Vamanos,*" Juan repeated and the pickup bolted towards U.S. Interstate 8. Two border agents and one Zeta could not hear the command. The husband and wife could and wept. They were only about one hundred yards from the truck when the wheels jerked and spit gravel into the air. They knew that when the sun came up they would be caught and returned to Mexico.

Abdul was impressed. This was an organization to know; they were professional.

The cool air passing over the truck caused shivers to run across the now sweaty bodies, but no one cared. They were riding – and they were in America! They huddled down low against the wind and close to each other for warmth in the bed of the pickup. Suddenly the bumpy ride ended as the driver turned onto the road Juan had mentioned. No one mentioned the bodies or the people left behind. On the paved road, the truck picked up speed. An hour later, the driver turned again onto a major highway – U.S. Interstate 8. In the limited moonlight, Abdul saw a blue shield sign with the number 8 in the middle. Then he saw a sign which read: TRAVEL CAUTION. ILLEGAL IMMIGRATION AND SMUGGLING MAY BE ENCOUNTERED IN THIS AREA. He read it again. *If they know enough to put up signs, why do they not do something about it? Are the Americans as stupid as we have been told?*

At breakfast the following morning, Johnny Bezzos grabbed the remote control and tuned the TV to a local news channel. "Good morning, New Orleans," the announcer began. "At the top of the news this morning is another tragedy along the Arizona border. Two border agents were killed in a shootout with what appears to be Mexican bandits. Their bodies were found early this morning after being spotted by a helicopter fly-over. Many local residents are asking why two agents would be out alone at night without sufficient backup. A spokesperson for Homeland Security has said there was no need for them to be out there alone The spokesperson further stated that even with this incident, the border is currently the most secure it has ever been. The district chief will hold a news conference at noon and we'll keep you informed. In other news..."

Click. Johnny turned off the TV. "Ya know," he said. "I have a buddy who told me that those guys have their hands tied by all the government regulations. Sometimes the agents have just had enough, so they go out on their own to try and stop this flood of illegals. They get no support from the higher-ups. I sure hope the organization takes care of their families. They damn sure didn't take care of their people."

"But why were there out there alone? I heard the Secretary of Homeland Security say that they were out there on their own." Melinda was puzzled.

"They sure were. Anyone who tries to do the job they're supposed to do and thinks the government will support them, those folks are already on their own," Johnny replied. "Lots of folks believe in some kinda – I think far out conspiracy bit. They think the government really wants to force us into an alliance kinda like in Europe – make the U.S., Mexico, and Canada become almost one nation. The conspiracy folks say it's a move towards 'Global Governance,' so the government wants the borders open. They actually resent these guys who try to enforce the laws. I don't know. Hell, I don't even understand the stuff I think I know. Life wasn't this complicated on the farm."

"And what do they mean that the border is now safer than it has ever been?" Melinda wanted to know.

"Honey," Johnny answered, "who was that guy who said that 'if you tell a lie, make it big enough, and tell it often enough... the more you tell it, the more people will begin to believe it.' Our government has obviously read more Machiavelli than they have the Constitution."

In Phoenix, the travelers were dropped off on the outskirts of town and huddled into a makeshift barn. Juan and his Zetas disappeared immediately, leaving the travelers somewhat bewildered. However, soon other guides appeared, calling each person by name and taking them away, individually, in other vehicles. They had not been there long when a man called to both Abdul and the other Muslim. It was their guide – the person who would coordinate the next phase of their travels in the long process of their mission. Abdul was headed for Washington, D.C. to help train a small group of suicide bombers and his handler had decided to have him travel by Amtrak, rather than by air. It would only take three days longer and there was no rush. This plan allowed him to avoid any possible "no-fly" problems; however, the train ride caused some concern for Abdul. The train passed through four days of breathtakingly beautiful country and the service on the train was such as he had never thought possible. *Why has Allah allowed these infidels to live so well and with so much abundance? Why are there so many fat Americans? In my country, only the very wealthy are fat. Here, almost everyone is fat. Why does Allah allow this?* he questioned, but then he'd catch himself and promise extra prayers for his impure thoughts. It was not his place to question Allah. His place was to obey the commands of Allah and the Fatwa to kill the infidels. He would strike a great blow against the great Satan. He would honor his parents by becoming a martyr. His family would have a great celebration in his honor. Friends and neighbors would honor his family. It was a future he wished for dearly. He focused and concentrated on not allowing such impure thoughts to enter into his mind but it was difficult. The train was air-conditioned. There was ample food and drink, but best of all, there were no flies. Each time he would eat, he would recall the flies. *Where are they?* he asked himself. And then he would force himself to think of something else. It was difficult. Was he feeling a sense of envy for America and Americans? No! That could not be. Resentment was a better word.

Eleven

"Somewhere in China"

In a remote location somewhere near the Three Gorges Dam on the Yangtze River, Jinjing Wu called her senior staff together. In Chinese, "Jinjing" means "bright and clear." It described her well. Her mind was quick and uncluttered. She could easily grasp the most profound concepts and she had a clear vision of where she wanted to be. She was a fervent Chinese Nationalist.

"Today we have reached a milestone," she began. "Thanks to the work of our operatives in both Canada and America, we are within striking distance of success. We have an operative who will soon have information on the NASA equipment. This should allow us access to the American's Space Administration and to their Missile Defense Systems." Ms. Wu was the head of a select group of scientists, electronics engineers, mathematicians, and computer experts who were working a mission of great importance to China. They were developing a sophisticated computer virus: a computer worm capable of damaging the United States' Missile Defense System, as well as major portions of America's electrical power grid. The process was simple enough, but extremely difficult to build. It was referred to as "The Golden Dragon."

First, the team had to understand what components to attack. Although not complete, much of this aspect had been accomplished by the ChIS, through operatives such as Fred Ming Yao, who had been helping to identify the manufacturers of various components of the computers and operating systems necessary for successful deployment of America's Anti-Missile Defense. Ms. Wu was confident that the equipment used by NASA would be common to many of the military defense missile systems. Once Yao, or some other operative, identified the manufacturers, she knew they would have entree into the U.S. classified systems. They could then infect and cripple the U.S. system.

Second, they had to develop a computer worm (virus) that could enter the defense network, travel from computer to computer totally unobserved until it found the specific system it wanted to target, and to then lie dormant and undetected until activated. This had taken several years. It could have taken much longer, but they had learned much from their analysis of the Stuxnet virus which had done exactly that, causing severe damage to the Iranian nuclear plants in 2008 to 2010. Although not yet in the final stages, Jinjing Wu was confident that success was near.

Third, they had to develop the entry into the United States' Defense System. This was the easiest and simplest of the three tasks. When ready, Yao and other operatives would unleash multiple worms through multiple sources and then let the worms find their way into the U.S. defense and power grid systems to await the activation signal from China. Additionally, the worm could be introduced unwittingly by workers in the United States government. The Chinese would plant the virus in several commercial Chinese websites where it would be harmless until some curious American would log onto one of these Chinese websites and unknowingly infect their personal computer. Following the concept of "Six Degrees of Separation," the virus would spread throughout America, harmless, until it found the specific targets for which it was built. One likely scenario: An ordinary citizen checks a Chinese website and his/her personal computer would then be infected. That person exchanges emails with any number of friends, anyone of whom may be related to a

U.S. government employee, infecting their computers. Eventually, the government employee brings work home – even unclassified information or data via a flash drive. His or her computer is infected from the email and now the flash drive is infected. When the employee returns to work and reuses the flash drive, the virus is introduced into the governmental system, eventually finding the way into the Missile Defense System. This "breaching of the wall" is designed to occur multiple times, thus infecting and compromising the entire system. Ms. Wu and her team were counting on the lax security of the U.S. to make this part easy to accomplish and Yao's contacts would allow him to gain access to either NASA or the FAA. When China decides it is time to openly establish world dominance, the worm is to be activated. All United States Missile Defense Systems will be disabled, as well as major portions of the U.S. power grids. Disabling the power grids will reduce the ability of the U.S. Military to implement secondary command and control.

Ms. Wu was fond of saying, "If they cannot talk – they cannot implement or execute. Their defense will be useless." China's long range missiles would then be free to strike – unopposed - anywhere in the United States: Nuclear Armageddon. And, if necessary, the Iranian missiles being installed in Venezuela might also be utilized. Most Chinese analysts felt that launch of the missiles would never be required. Their dominant belief was that when faced with such a specter of defeat, the cowardly American government would merely capitulate.

Pleased with her team's progress, Ms. Wu stepped outside onto the balcony of her laboratory overlooking the Three Gorges Dam on the Yangtze River. She smiled as she looked out at the majestic view of massive rocky cliffs rising above Asia's longest river, thinking about what she and her team had accomplished. For millennia, the Yangtze had ravaged the area, uncontrolled. *China's people and their ingenuity have conquered the wild river. It is the largest and most powerful river in Asia, but we have conquered it and are now using its mighty power.* The dream expressed half a century ago by Chairman Mao was now a reality. In his poem Mao had written, "The dam will cut through the clouds and rain of the Wuxi Gorge, and a smooth lake will appear amid the deep canyons." *It is as he predicted*, she thought. The dam was a masterpiece of Chinese engineering – the largest hydroelectric plant in the world. *This entire project is Chinese. We did not have to bring in foreigners and their ideas. Soon China will rightfully be master of the entire world. We will bring the arrogant Americans to their knees.* She smiled as she surveyed the massive beauty before her. *It is our destiny.*

Department of Homeland Security

"So, how are we doing? The Secretary for Homeland Security addressed his top scientists and engineers.

"Sir, as you know, we have over 2500 network connections used every day by millions of federal workers around the world. We thought we had a secure system until Stuxnet and Wikileaks. We believe Stuxnet was developed by friendly nations, but our intelligence has been unable to verify the source. We are only thankful that it delayed the Iranian development of nuclear weapons. But, God help us if our enemies can get it."

"Yes, but if these so-called 'friendly nations' can develop this, then so can our enemies. Why can't we find the source?"

"Sir, the system is too sophisticated. We cannot crack it – or trace it. Actually, it seems the entire world would like to know who built the damn thing – and how they got it past all of the Iranian cyber-security."

"I don't accept that!" the Secretary nearly shouted. "I want the source! This is like the first weaponized computer virus ever built. It is a game-changer in the security business. If we get caught behind, it's Katie-Bar-The-Door time for this country. Someone could destroy our nuclear defense systems. Do you realize what that means? To all of us! We better damn well solve this now!" The veins pulsed on the neck of the Secretary.

"Yes, Sir. We'll keep working until we solve this, but, we're not the only ones trying to solve this. It appears that the actual virus is the most sophisticated ever encountered. We'd better hope and pray that we get our cyber defense in order before someone like Russia or China develops something similar."

"Are there any new indications of anyone – friendly or otherwise—trying to sabotage our secure networks?"

"Sir, we have massive hacker activity every day. This isn't just how to keep out the Stuxnet type viruses, since Wikileaks, we have to have better control over access. We're working day and night on the new Einstein 2 and Einstein 3 networks. They should be operational soon and as you know, they'll all be guarded by highly sophisticated anti-intrusion detection and prevention programs. If we can just hold off any successful large-scale attacks on our systems for another year, we'll be secure. Right now we're in a difficult short-term deficit."

"What's taking so long to make them operational?"

"Sir, as you know, progress has been extremely slow because of privacy issues, technology issues, and complexity of contracts. The ACLU has already filed one lawsuit over privacy issues. The judge made us halt everything until that was resolved, which took about fourteen months."

"Don't they know this is a serious national security issue?"

"Sir, apparently that is not their concern."

"So they would rather see us attacked by China or Russia or some Jihadist outfit?"

"That's not for me to say, but if you want my personal opinion, it appears to me that's exactly what they want.

"What the hell is this country coming to? What about our allies? Are they working on solutions?"

"Hard to say. Again, since Wikileaks not many of our friends trust us enough to give us any information. They just don't trust us with their security. They won't even discuss it with us. When we try to talk to them, they just turn away and shake their heads. When we let that Wikileaks thing happen, we caused severe damage to a lot of our friends and most of them haven't recovered from it yet. They think we're sloppy with our intel. They think we've grown complacent. And worse yet, our CIA operatives around the world will no longer risk detaining terrorist suspects. Those folks in the

Department of Justice are prosecuting more CIA agents than terrorists these days, so we get less and less intelligence. Nobody trusts us – or believes us."

"Hell," answered the Secretary. "They're right! I don't trust us anymore either! How can we go from having the greatest security in the world to being the laughing stock of every intel agency? Tell me."

"Sir, we just got lax."

"Damn straight we did and our kids will suffer for it. Keep me posted."

"Sir, have you informed the President of this latest situation?"

That's where I'm headed right after I leave here."

The engineers all returned to their work. They now knew that they were more important to America's national security than an additional division of soldiers and marines. It was critical for them to re-establish our security systems as the best in the world. No if, ands, or buts!

Twelve

"The FBI and Homeland Security"

"Please have a seat." The Senior FBI Field Agent for New Orleans motioned Sam Spade towards a chair.

"Thanks." Sam pulled the chair up to the desk and sat down.

"So what can the FBI do for you, today?" the agent asked.

"Well," Sam began. "I don't know if this comes under terrorism, cyber crime, public corruption, or what, but I think we have a problem and I believe it falls under your purview."

"Sounds pretty bad. What's this all about?"

"I have reason to believe that a prominent politician is helping Chinese operatives get classified information on our governmental internet systems."

"That's a pretty serious charge. Do you have data to back it up?"

"I believe we have enough to warrant the FBI getting involved."

"So what do you have?"

Sam produced the papers and data he had collected during his investigation. "I went as far on this as I thought reasonable, then decided it was best to turn it all over to you. I sincerely hope there's nothing going on here, but figured it was best to let you folks take a look and decide what, if anything, needs to be done."

"That was a smart idea," the agent replied. He spent several minutes looking through the papers. "It will take us awhile to go through all of this. Will you be in the area for a few days? If we need any clarification or additional information, I'd like to be able to contact you quickly."

"Absolutely," Sam replied. "Here's my card and all my contact info is also on the cover page of the report. I live here in town."

A week later, Sam was asked to go to FBI Headquarters in Washington, D.C. Sam parked his car and looked around. In front of him was the entrance to the J. Edgar Hoover Building, the world famous home of the FBI. It's an impressive-looking building, commanding the view along Pennsylvania Ave. He entered the lobby, presented his identification to security, and then waited until an escort arrived and led him to the meeting room. Waiting there were representatives from the FBI's Counter-Terrorism Taskforce and Cyber Crimes Division. Additionally, a senior representative from the Department of Homeland Security's Cyber Security and Communications Integration Center had joined the group at the request of the FBI.

As soon as everyone was seated, the meeting leader began. "Mr. Spade," how did you obtain this material? Who else knows about it?"

Sam explained that in his capacity as an auditor/inspector for the State of Louisiana some irregularities had been brought to his attention and he had investigated them. "When it reached the point that it appeared to be larger than just a Louisiana problem, my boss and I decided to bring you guys into the loop as quickly and as quietly as possible."

"We're glad you did," an agent interrupted. "The Chinese — among others – have been trying to get access to all of our national systems. It is getting tougher and tougher to protect against the attacks. The idea that one of our leaders would be selling us out is tough to swallow."

"Wait a minute," Sam spoke up. "I'm not ready to accuse the Senator. What we need is for the FBI to decide if it is worth pursuing—and if so, to go after it. I'm just bringing in the information. But, I do think there's something wrong. I'm not qualified to investigate further than I already have."

"We understand," said another agent. "We've been shut down on several operations because it pissed off some politician. This could be big time. We want to check it out and we want to keep it quiet until we know for sure if there's a problem. We'll protect you while we conduct the investigation. You did the right thing."

"If we need help," asked another, "can we count on you?"

"Damn straight," Sam replied.

"Good, thanks."

The agent then addressed the representative from Homeland Security. "Any thoughts?"

"You bet." Have you guys ever heard of Stuxnet?" Most indicated they had. "Well, we still believe it was the Israelis who put it together. They did one helluva job. Threw the Iranian nuclear efforts way off stride. The Israelis won't admit or deny it – they just grin when we question them; but whoever developed it, this is a game-changer. Remember when we thought we were the top dogs in the space race and then the Russians put up Sputnik?" The assemblage all nodded. "Well that was the kick in the butt we needed to get going on space. The Russians were kicking our butts and we didn't even know it! We were so damn smug – thought we were miles ahead of everybody, but that was all about image and propaganda. All we lost was some short-term prestige. Then we went to work and kicked *their* asses. We became king in space. However, this is real danger. If someone can shut down our missile defense systems—even for a few hours, it leaves us open to nuclear attack – *massive* attack. And to make the cheese even more binding, ever since Wikileaks none of our allies trust us with classified documents and information. Even if they know positively that something's going down they're reluctant to share that info with us. Our butts are really hanging out here! If this guy is in bed with Chinese operatives, we need to shut him down right now!"

A few days later a special task force was convened to investigate Senator Matthew Tibideaux of Louisiana.

"Christ!" One agent complained as the group assembled. "Our agents are spread razor thin all across the country trying to preempt these damn jihadist bombers. We've already stopped three of them this year alone. Who knows how many more are out there? Doesn't anyone higher up realize that if we go slack here one of these guys will get through? Why in hell are we gonna pull agents off this to put surveillance on some damn politician? What'd he do, screw some movie star's wife?"

"Naw," a burly agent sneered. "In our Congress, they don't screw somebody's *wife,* they screw each other! Haven't you heard? Congress has its own 'Don't Ask, Don't Tell' policy!" That got him a big laugh from everybody.

"Yeah," added another. "Did you hear that someone tried to get the TSA to provide the same security for Congress they were doing at the airports? You know, the extra pat-downs and stuff? Especially after that one Congresswoman got shot. Somebody thought we needed extra protection for that bunch. I think the American people are the ones who need protection – from the politicians."

"Yeah," the first agent. "Back to the TSA and the pat-downs. It seems two Congressmen kept getting back in line and made Congress two hours late starting work while these two got their jollies from the pat-down!" Laughter filled the room.

"Awright! Enough already, knock it off," the agent-in-charge snapped. "Time to get serious. Now back to business. I understand what you're saying, but if the information we have is true, the damage could be a thousand times more dangerous than any suicide bomber. This could affect our entire defense system."

The protestor nodded and mumbled to himself, "Yeah and one of these days soon some damn home-grown jihadist will slip past us because we're spread so thin."

"You got something else on your mind?" the senior agent asked.

"Yeah, can we get some help on this? Or maybe get more information out to the public to be more watchful?"

"Well, that would be nice," another agent added, "but the American people don't give a shit. Nobody thinks it can happen to them, so they just ignore any threats. Everyone's too busy with their personal lives. Remember that Israeli security guy who did the experiment for us? You know, the guy who left the briefcases in a bunch of public places: Grand Central Station, a major airport, a shopping mall. I think he had half a dozen out. *No one reported them* – not even one. They all just sat there for over two hours except for the one in the train station because some doofus tried to steal it! But nobody reported them as suspicious. The Israeli guy said people in Israel would be screaming within five minutes. That's why they aren't getting these damn bombers blowing themselves up inside Israel. Americans are too complacent. One's gonna slip through someday soon and there will be hell to pay."

"Hey, Charlie," someone added. "You think we're spread thin? How many cities have had to lay off a bunch of cops because of their budgets? We won't be getting a lot of help from the state and local guys. Hell, they're already having a tough time."

"Yeah, but we still have enough money for the government to bring thousands of Hamas sympathizers into the country, given 'em free food, housing, plane rides—the works while we lay off cops."

"Yeah, we all agree," the leader added, "but our job is to protect the American people the best we can, regardless of their attitude and regardless of budgets. Now, Sam Spade here works in the office of the Inspector General for the Louisiana Department of Transportation. He's the one who first identified the irregularities. He'll brief us."

Sam briefed the group, filling them in on the investigation he had done. "Any questions?" he asked.

"No," someone replied, "but that's some mighty fine work. Nice job."

"Thanks. Any other comments?" There were none.

"So, here's the breakdown," the senior agent said. "Sam and his staff will be helping to identify additional data, plus some of our own agents are doing additional digging. We need to know more about this Future Technology outfit and the top people there. Additionally, we need to put a tail on the senator and his family. It'll be tough for several reasons, not the least of which is that he IS a senator, so we have to be especially careful. Also, it will require two separate details: one for D.C. and one for New Orleans. He goes home almost every weekend. I'm hoping that it's all just a misunderstanding and we can clean it up quickly, but, it's too sensitive to waste any more time. Any questions?

"So what exactly do we think he's doing? What's his purpose?"

"We don't know for sure – that's the problem. What we suspect is that he's selling access to classified information. He helps some Chinese outfit to get contracts with the government. We think the Chinese guy is then providing classified info to Chinese

Intelligence. What could be even worse is if these operatives are somehow connected to a Stuxnet-type virus."

"Damn!"

"Yeah! If it's true we need to cut his nuts off and stuff 'em down his throat," one agent mumbled.

"Ain't funny," a second responded. "Probably the most dangerous time in American history is when Congress is in session."

"Yeah!" Many heads nodded around the room.

"Hey, ya know," one agent stood up. "Maybe it's time for us to stop making jokes about these politicians. It isn't making them any better. All it's doing is dragging us down. So whaddya say? Let's work on the positive. Who's with me?" There was a long pause before another agent stood up.

"I think Bill's got a point. Regardless of our personal feelings, I think we should keep a positive attitude here at work."

"Besides," someone added. "All those jokes about politicians aren't really jokes anyway – they're all true!!!!"

"Okay, let's get to work – for real."

Thirteen

"Home-Grown Jihadists"

Unaware and unconcerned about the Secretary's meeting, numerous groups of men and - to a lesser degree - women were holding clandestine meetings across the country. Many were debating how to use the American legal and political system to insure that Sharia law becomes the law of the land in America. They were especially active in Michigan where they were not debating the merits of U.S. Constitutional law. They were taking active steps to destroy it, even if it took violence. Several camps had training sites where radicalized Muslims trained in military fashion. Although known to the police and the FBI, these sites could not be entered by authorities – or anyone else for that matter. America's laws protected them.

One group of Muslim Americans gathered in Baltimore, only a few, short miles away from the nation's capitol. Although most were American citizens, they called each other by Muslim names. Among them was a college drop-out originally born and raised as Jonathan Williams, who had grown up in a middle-income family in the metropolitan area.

Jonathan was a shy young man with few friends. In high school he spent hours upon hours playing X-box and other games. Occupied with his games, he had no need for friends, but occasionally he did feel lonely. After graduation, he enrolled in a local community college and planned to work as a computer programmer, where he hoped to design games like the ones he enjoyed playing. Secretly, he also hoped that once in college he would meet people like himself and then he'd have friends to "hang" with.

One afternoon while sitting under a tree on the campus lawn, a young man sat down next to him and asked what game he was playing. Jonathan showed the young man what he was doing and how to play the game. The young man introduced himself as Mohammed Kasim, produced his own DS game player with multiple games, and they spent an enjoyable afternoon together. It was the first time Jonathan had felt that he had a friend since middle school. They agreed to meet the following day and to play more games. Jonathan felt good and slept well that night.

The friendship grew quickly. Jonathan and his new friend, Kasim, had been meeting for about a week when Kasim asked if Jonathan knew anything about Islam.

"No," Jonathan laughed. "I don't know or care anything about any religion. That's just a bunch of crap. You come into this world, people treat you like crap, and then you die. I don't need religion."

"There's more to it than that," Kasim replied patiently. "You are correct about most religions, but Islam is different. You should come join our study group and see for yourself. Allah cares for each of us, but we must understand his ways."

Initially, Jonathan had considered the group meeting to be only social and he didn't pay much attention to what was being said. The fact that he had been asked to join the group was enough for him. He had friends and a place to go where there were other people who would talk with him, which was something new in his life. When they asked him to go with them to their mosque, he felt that he could not refuse. After all, they were the only people around who seemed to enjoy him for him.

At the mosque he listened to the many Muslims who were angry at U.S. policies around the world. They discussed the arrogance of America and how the ways of Americans had been detrimental to Islam. They prayed often for the rise of Sharia law and they were committed to seeing Sharia become the law of America. Soon, Jonathan was agreeing with their arguments that America had violated many countries, especially the countries of the Muslim world. America was the great Satan and had caused many Muslim families to suffer. "Why can't America leave us alone? Why must America be so arrogant?" many asked in their lamentations.

The meetings had become more vocal and more anti-American. They had accessed as many of the Islamic websites as possible for additional proof of the corruption of America. Jonathan was drawn to and fascinated by the films of jihad training. He especially enjoyed the violent scenes of suicide bombers and Muslim fire fights against the governmental forces of the world. *Wow! These are better than the fights on Game boxes. This is the real shit!* Far greater than his desire to be a martyr was his desire to play the real games.

Jonathan committed to travel to Yemen to study with the jihadist movement there. He was gathering the money for his trip when the group was visited by a young man names Zakir Abdul who claimed to be a member of Hamas. Abdul had only recently come to America by way of Mexico. He exhorted them to "Go forth for Allah." He encouraged them to learn how to make homemade bombs and to strike against the infidels. He was especially vocal following the release of the Wikileaks information cables. "See?" he exclaimed. "America is corrupting even the Muslim governments. Saudi Arabia is using American intelligence and weapons to attack other Muslims and so is the Yemeni government. America is fighting a war against Islam – and using Muslims to kill Muslims. We must make them suffer for these injustices."

The gathering of young men cheered him. With each meeting, Jonathan became more and more committed. Eventually, he converted to Islam. Converting to Islam gave meaning to his life. Just prior to his conversion ceremony, Jonathan was approached by Abdul.

"And what will be your new name?" asked Abdul.

Jonathan grinned widely and replied, "I have chosen 'Daib Babar.'"

"That is wonderful," Abdul responded. "Do you know what it means?"

"Yes," Daib responded. "It means 'the devoted lion'."

To him it symbolized and described his new life: one devoted to the cause of jihad and a lion in the execution of it. His conversion gave him a great sense of power. He had never been so committed to anything in his life. Here he was surrounded by his friends who were committed to the same cause. Finally, he belonged. The desire to become a martyr grew within him.

Eventually, he denounced his American family, severing all ties. He refused to accept calls from his mother and he returned all mail unopened, marked "Return to Sender." He declared to his new friends that he wished to become a martyr and to reside forever in heaven.

The young man from Hamas was pleased and was warm and friendly towards Daib, more so than anyone else had ever been. Daib excelled in the training. He especially enjoyed the instruction and training in the preparation of home-made bombs.

"I am prepared to go to Yemen to learn and to train amongst the brothers. I will return a warrior," Daib exclaimed to Zakir Abdul, the young man from Hamas.

Ironically, Abdul cautioned Jonathan and the others not to attempt contact with known Islamic extremists and not to travel to the Middle East. "The FBI and other American agencies are closely watching those whom they suspect are preparing for the triumph of Islam. The best weapon we have is secrecy," he was fond of saying. He also advised them to not do anything that looked even remotely suspicious. One member disobeyed and spent a weekend at one of the militant Islamic training centers in South Carolina.

Upon his return, Abdul was furious and ordered him to leave. He screamed at him, "Don't you realize that the FBI is watching these sites and they now have you on camera? You must leave before you jeopardize this group and our missions."

As the chastised youth left, Abdul turned to the others. "I am one of the greatest bomb-makers ever trained by Hamas. I will build your bombs, but you must each help me. Also you each need to decide how you want to transport your bomb. The explosive vest is the simplest and it is the easiest to hide."

Since 9/11/2001, the Department of Homeland Security and the FBI had instituted a massive campaign to stop attacks on American soil. A major tool in their success at stopping these isolated attacks had been the tracking mechanisms – identifying those people traveling to radical Muslim locations – both here in America and abroad. More importantly, the Department of Homeland Security had coordinated and incorporated all possible federal, state, and local governmental agencies into a highly coordinated "internal spy" operation. The core of the program was the request for all Americans to report suspicious activity. These Suspicious Activity Reports (SARs) had resulted in the accumulation of large-scale information caches and data on ordinary citizens. This information was maintained at the J. Edgar Hoover building in

Washington on people who had never committed any crimes but merely looked suspicious. There were also a number of locations called "fusion centers" in virtually every city in America. Enormous amounts of data were stored in the centers. Most of it was unrelated to any crimes; it was merely a growing collection of data on the American people. "Big Brother" was not even sure what to do with this information and most Americans had no idea that so much of their personal data was catalogued and stored in government vaults.

However, the process did force these home-grown jihadists to change their methods of operation and to seek local assistance. Daib Babar and his companions trained for many months to build and conceal their bombs and they'd done so without any advice from outside of the United States – with the exception of help from Zakir Abdul. The Internet provided them with access to all of the information they needed. Supplies were easily obtained and Abdul was well-versed in the construction of bombs.

Each vest bomb that he built contained approximately fifteen pounds of explosive, framed around the wearer's body. Around the outside Abdul inserted several pounds of loose nails and steel ball-bearings. He told them that when the device detonated, anyone within fifteen feet of it would have less than a ten percent chance of surviving. He'd constructed many for Hamas. He was most diligent in their instruction.

The numbers of Muslim extremists had grown to such proportions that they were now largely autonomous, although spread across most of the land. Jonathan's group was soon comfortable with their bombs and so selected the time and location of their attacks: Washington, D.C. and the metro area during the National Cherry Blossom Festival. Daib had been selected to detonate his bomb at the largest concert to be held during the National Cherry Blossom Festival which made him extremely proud.

The selection also allowed him to carry his bomb in something other than a vest. He had chosen his guitar case because the vest made him itchy and sweaty. Also, since his bomb was being carried inside the case, it could be a bit larger and more dangerous. Daib's chest swelled with the pride of importance. He was delighted to be able to use his guitar case. He swore to Allah, *I will be a true mujahedeen. I will strike the infidels with joy in my heart!*

Two other locations had been selected for the same day: the Montgomery Mall in Bethesda, Maryland and the Amtrak Union Station in Washington. Abdul had selected Union Station as the site of his attack. He and his friends would all enter Heaven together. Daib soon would play the greatest game of his life. He was filled with anticipation.

Fourteen

"Happy on the Bayou"

Tibideaux boarded the New Orleans flight and took his seat in first class. Shortly thereafter an FBI agent boarded, taking the first seat in back of first class. From his seat the agent had an unobstructed view of the Senator, who was returning home a day early so as to attend a fundraiser in his hometown. His wife met him at the airport and they drove directly home. The FBI agent was met by an associate from the New Orleans office and together they followed the senator and his wife home. They waited outside, across and down the street, keeping an eye on the house.

The kids were in school, so Tibideaux and his wife sat at the kitchen table and had a cup of coffee. After a few minutes spent catching up on the happenings since he was last home, Matthew decided that the time was right.

"Honey, what do you think about me running for Governor?"

"Well, at least you'd be home more," she replied.

"I'm serious." He pushed.

"Me too," she grinned." I guess I'd have to think about it. Why?"

"Well, I think I could really help the people of Louisiana. We need stronger leadership and I think I can bring more jobs."

"Well, the state could certainly use the jobs," she replied.

"Right!" He practically shouted. "And tomorrow at the ceremony I'll have two big job announcements that will be dynamite."

"Really? What?"

"Well, I managed to get the administration to do a partial lifting of the ban on drilling in the Gulf. The EPA won't officially announce it until next week, but I've been cleared to announce the possibility tomorrow."

"That's great! How many jobs do you think that could provide?" Nicole was excited. Everyone knew how important the oil jobs were to the local economy. "I'm really proud of you," she said, "but I'm still hoping that someday you will help me run the business, then we could be together all the time."

"I'm hoping several hundred – maybe even more," he said, ignoring her comment about the restaurants. "Then I'm going to announce the opening of a new plant with almost a hundred technology jobs. It'll be a big day."

"Matthew, that's great," she squealed. She came around the table and hugged his neck. "Wonderful! Congratulations!"

"Thanks," he grinned.

"Now, I have another question," she said, fully aware of that he'd dodged her question about the family business. She intended to bring it up again later, but for now she wanted them to all enjoy the weekend.

"Shoot," he replied.

"Okay. You promised that Saturday would be strictly a family day, so I've made plans for us to spend the day on the Atchafalaya. What do you think?"

"Honey, that's great!" he answered. "We haven't been together on the river for years. That's great!" He leaned back in his chair, smiling. He did miss the family outings and was hoping this would fill the void.

The following evening, Senator Tibideaux made his announcements at an event to raise funds for a children's hospital. "Now," he cautioned, "the administration has told me that the ban will require some additional inspections, but as each well meets the safety inspection, that well will be allowed to resume operations – immediately." He was interrupted by applause. "And, we'll also be bringing a new technology company into this parish. This should provide approximately one hundred new jobs in technology." He grinned broadly as he was again interrupted by applause.

"Senator," a reporter stood and shouted. "When will these new jobs actually be available?"

"Within the year," he replied, now assuming a serious visage.

"And when do you anticipate the hiring will occur?"

"That will be up to the contractor, but I assure you, they are as anxious as we are."

"Senator," another reporter waved his hand. "Have you and Mr. Bezzos resolved your differences?"

The Senator stiffened momentarily at the mention of Bezzos' name and replied in measured tones. "I choose not to comment on these petty matters. Mr. Bezzos has his beliefs. I have mine. But know this – the jobs we are discussing now are proof that as your Senator I am fighting every day for the citizens of the great state of Louisiana. Thank you." He left the stage and immediately departed for home.

The family was up early the next morning and headed towards the river. The Atchafalaya River is one of America's most beautiful, exciting, and mysterious national treasures. It is the largest active river delta on the North American continent. Scenery along the banks is ever-changing and breathtaking. One moment you'll float past great grassy marshes and sunken logs with perhaps an alligator or two warily watching your movement. The next you'll glide past beautiful, majestic cypress trees that are several hundred years old. Nearby will be a decaying stump of an ancient cypress and resting on it will be a great-horned owl. The banks may be lined with sugarcane or palmettos and filled with wading birds.

The Atchafalaya is home to over 270 species of birds. It's also the largest nesting area for wading birds in America. Wildlife abounds, living off the land as they have forever, except for the raccoon vigorously chewing on a Big Mac and fries left by some slob who litters even amidst such beauty. You may pass an area of historic live oaks, beautifully draped with Spanish moss, growing near to a clump of Tupelo gum trees. For Nicole and Nadine the trip was merely for relaxation and enjoying nature's beauty. It had been quite some time since they'd been on the water together and they were constantly pointing out sightings to each other, especially the multitude of birds.

"Oh look, babies!" Nicole would shout.

"Where?" Nadine would ask and then point her camera at the area her mother indicated, taking picture after picture of families of birds. Most of the birds ignored them, but occasionally one would stretch its neck to watch them.

Matthew and Gary were avid fishermen. Gary had always felt closer to his father while fishing than at any other time in his life. Only then did they seem to have anything in common and Matthew did not constantly criticize his son. Matthew would fill with pride each time Gary hooked another "keeper" size bass. "Nice job," he'd say and Gary would beam. When they went fishing, Gary always left his Game Box in the car.

Nicole had contracted with an old family friend, a local fishing guide named Vincent, to take them out on his boat. Boating and fishing on the Atchafalaya can be difficult because of the shifting shallows and sunken logs. You need someone familiar with the water to avoid getting stranded. Vincent had been a guide all his life – or so it seemed – and knew how to find the "good" water for fishing. And, like most Louisiana fishermen, he had tales to tell.

"Now, be keerful," he cautioned. "Don' know what might be in de water, so watch out. Las' week, bin fishin' wid Boudreaux and Guidry – two my pals. We runs outta bait. Think we gonna hafta go back in. Then Boudreaux look over de boat. He see dis big watamoccasin snake wid a frog in his mout." Vincent held up his hand, shaping it to represent a snake's mouth. "Now, I tell you, we all knows dat you cut up dat frog, he fo sure be good fishin' bait. So Boudreaux reach over and cotched that snake back behind he head and bring him into de boat. Den he try to get dat frog from dat snake mout, but that snake won' leggo dat frog no matter how much Boudreaux fight him.

"Then Guidry gots a idee. He pull out his bottle of homemade Lusiana likker and pour it into dat snake mout. Dat snake, he gag on dat likker and squirm lak crazy, then spit out dat frog. Guidry grab de frog. Boudreaux tro' dat snake back in de water and we do some good fishing wid dat frog cut up fo' bait. Then when we was goin' home, Boudreaux feel sumpin' tappin' on his leg. He look down, and guess what?"

"What?" Tibideaux asked with a grin.

"Well," Vincent continued. "It be dat snake – wid TWO frog in he mout! I guess he like that homemade likker! He wanna make a trade!" Vincent grinned as big as the bayou as the Tibideaux family all laughed.

"Aw, c'mon," Gary laughed. "You expect us to believe that? That's a joke, right?"

Vincent laughed. "Jes funnin' you, Gary... jes funnin'."

It was a great day on the river and Matthew truly relaxed for the first time in months. Nicole and Nadine were constantly pointing out and photographing different birds and mammals. Gary was the happiest of all. He caught two huge largemouth bass, one of which was large enough that Vincent named him "Ol' Bucketmout'.

No one noticed the boat with a guide and two men dressed more for a boardroom meeting than for a day on the river. The two men had cautioned their guide to follow Vincent's boat, but discreetly and at a good distance. Although uncomfortable in their "city" clothes, they enjoyed the beauty of the river.

The Atchafalaya seemed especially busy that Saturday. There were many other families out on the water that day, among them were Johnny and Melinda Bezzos. Johnny loved the water and had spent many happy days fishing throughout Louisiana, but the Atchafalaya was his favorite. There was such a large variety of fish. However, on this Saturday he was not fishing. He'd promised Melinda a relaxing day on the water, doing nothing but enjoying the day and he was keeping his promise.

"How ya' doin'?" he asked.

"This is really relaxing." She stretched out on the cushions he'd arranged for her as he expertly guided the skiff along the banks of a small bayou.

"Honey," she asked. "Have you thought anymore about running again... for senator, I mean. You know, since our last talk?"

"That's a tough one," he replied. "May not have a choice, what with the economy and all. We just may not have enough money to run again. We've already used up more of our retirement money than I wanted to – and unless I can get a few more building contracts, we just might not be able to afford it."

"But, do you want to?" she insisted.

"Don't really know. I just feel that we need to get some elected officials who will really listen to us and we need to put serious term limits on all of 'em. Even the really good ones have a tough time staying clean after a coupla years."

Melinda lowered her hand into the water.

"Hey! Don't do that!" Johnny yelled at her.

"Do what?"

"Put your hand in the water like that, it's dangerous – snakes and gators. I ever tell you about the two guys caught the snake with a bullfrog in his mouth and took it from him for bait?"

"Johnny, Johnny, Johnny," she laughed. "That's the oldest joke in Louisiana."

He grinned and aimed the boat at a group of wading birds. A few of them lifted off and flew away, but most merely moved aside, watching the boat glide by.

Melinda rose and moved to the console. "Let me take it for awhile. You go back there and relax. Light up a cigar or something."

Johnny liked the idea. "Why thanks, Babe."

He left the wheel, poured them both a drink, then lit his cigar and stretched out on the back cushions. Melinda steered the boat as you would expect from someone with as many years of experience as she had.

That night the senator's family ate at one of the family restaurants where the chef prepared Gary's bass. It was delicious. They'd also hired a local Cajun band to play at the restaurant that night. They'd cleared a small open area where they could dance and many of the customers joined in.

Folks in Louisiana love to dance and when the fiddle and the accordion start putting out the beat it's difficult to sit still. Even Gary got up and danced when the band broke into "When the Saints Go Marchin' In." Although Gary wasn't a football player himself, he was a great fan of the New Orleans Saints. Matthew and Nicole danced the waltz and the two-step until closing time. Colossus never showed up.

For the two FBI agents it was an uneventful day – and night. They did enjoy the Crawfish Pie at Nicole's restaurant, as well as watching the dancing. Several times the local agent caught himself tapping his toes to the beat.

Johnny and Melinda ate raw oysters in a small shack on the river, washing them down with a pitcher of cold beer. Then they sat on the porch and watched the moon climb up, cascading its reflection on the water, sending shimmers across the bayou. It was late when they returned home to cuddle together in their bed.

The Tibideaux family attended early mass and then had a relaxing family day. Father and son argued how each considered the best way to catch bass. Gary, having proven himself the day before felt competent to debate the issue with his father. It had been a long time since he'd felt this close to his Dad.

That night as they prepared for bed, Nicole grabbed Matthew's hand. "I've got a question for you," she whispered.

"Really, what?"

"Instead of running for office again, why not come home and help me run the business? You've done your duty. We had such a great time this weekend. I'd just like to do this more often."

Matthew paused and reflected on the weekend. "Yes," he said, "this was a great weekend. It would be nice to do more like this. Let me think about it, okay?"

"That's a first step." She smiled and kissed him. They fell onto the bed in each other's arms.

Monday, the Senator boarded his flight for the return to Washington. He took his seat in first class and then reached into his briefcase to remove some paperwork to review. As he did so, Andy Micah, the FBI agent from D.C., boarded and walked past him. The Senator closed the briefcase and sat back in his seat. *Do I know this guy? He looks familiar.* The man continued into the coach section and sat down. *I know I've seen him before, but where?*

Puzzled, he searched his memory, but he couldn't clearly identify the man, so he concentrated on the briefing papers for next week's committee meeting when he wasn't thinking about how much he'd enjoyed the weekend. *Would be nice to be able to do this more often*, he thought. *Maybe I should consider giving it all up.* But then he thought about the pleasure of the "packages" and thought maybe he should give it just one more year. And, of course, the fact still remained that the State of Louisiana needed him was also a factor to be considered. *It's nice to feel needed.*

As Matthew reflected on his life, Sam Spade got a call.

"Hey, Sam. This is Joe Scorso. Remember me?"

"Sure do," Sam replied. "Been awhile. I thought you'd gone off the radar after our last meeting. What's up?"

"Listen, I don't have a lot of time, but I think I have something else you need to be aware of."

"Okay, what?" Sam asked.

"Well, I overheard Yao and Guifei talkin'. They still don't know that I understand a bit of Chinese. They were talkin' 'bout some 'stuxnet' thing. I didn't know what it was, so I went on the Internet. It's a real bitch in the cyber world and Yao is working on getting into that NASA contract. Man, this would be like that old Trojan Horse story. We need to break this thing up. Did you go to the FBI?"

"Yeah, they're working on it as we speak. But, thanks for this info. I'll pass this along."

"Do you think the Senator has any idea what's goin' on?" Joe asked. "Damn, I sure hope not."

"Hard to say," Sam answered. "But, I'll get this out to the FBI right away. Anything else?"

"God, I hope not. Gotta go." *Click.* Joe closed his cell phone.

"Shit," Sam muttered, and then called his New Orleans FBI contact.

Fifteen

"Springtime in Washington"

Back in Washington, Matthew took a cab to his apartment, unaware of the two men following him.

"So, anything go down out there?" Bob Jones asked his partner, Andy Micah.

"No," replied Andy Micah, the agent who had traveled to Louisiana. "Typical political stuff, for the most part. Ever been on the Atchafalaya River?

"The what?"

"The Atchafalaya River. It's beautiful. Might even go there next year on vacation."

"Hell, I thought you were going to tell me a joke. That's a big name." "Yeah, he took the family out for the day. Really nice."

"So now that you think he's a family man, you gonna be okay on this surveillance?"

"Oh, yeah, no problem. Seems like a nice family. Anything happen here?"

"Well, I put one of those GPS locators inside the wheel well. So if he goes anywhere, we can track him."

"Good."

Senator Tibideaux quickly immersed himself in the business of being a senator – making calls, studying proposals, and politicking in general. He worked tirelessly on several projects and proposals designed to bring some relief to the many unemployed across the nation. He knew that whatever relief he could muster nationwide would surely also ease the pain in Louisiana. Often, in quiet moments, he thought about Nicole's request. *It would be wonderful to spend more time with the family and to be back in Louisiana. Is all this really worth it?* Soon those thoughts were interrupted by memories of his "package" moments. He smiled and then filed the thoughts away. *The money could help me become Governor and then I could really help my people. I'd be a hero in the state. Maybe, if I just run for one more term... make my mark, so to speak, and then retire.* It was a pleasant thought.

Eventually, he returned to his work as a Senator. There were many actions pending on "the Hill" and the activity kept him fully occupied. He was too involved to even watch television so he didn't know that the murder of the MS-13 gang leader had initiated a vicious gang war within the capitol. Shootings were occurring so often that many residents began to believe they'd been transported to some old Western movie. For several weeks, he led a boring life. It was even more boring for the two FBI agents; however, they kept him under surveillance because that was their job as spring came to Washington – and with it the cherry blossoms.

Many years ago, the city of Tokyo presented a gift of approximately 3,000 cherry trees to the city of Washington, D.C. Since then, the trees have multiplied and today there are nearly 4,000 cherry trees in the nation's capitol. In the spring they present a magnificent sight throughout the city where their fragrant and vibrant pale pink and white flowers encourage a mood of happiness and tranquility as they herald the arrival of warmer weather. Tourists come from around the world to see them bloom, highlighting so many of our national monuments. One of the most beautiful sights in America is how these gorgeous trees frame the Jefferson Memorial around the tidal basin.

In honor of their blooming and the arrival of spring, each year the city holds the National Cherry Blossom Festival. The Festival lasts for two weeks and involves numerous festivities. Some of the most popular events for the Festival are held at the Sylvan Theater, an outdoor amphitheater at the corner of 15th Street and Independence Avenue near the northwest corner of the Washington Monument.

The second weekend of the Festival the Committee organized a concert at the Theater. The featured act was to be the Slam Dunks, a hip hop/heavy metal band that was the current favorite of millions of teenagers. Matthew didn't care much for their music, but they were unique in that every member had played in the NBA. These cross skills added to their teenage appeal, while he still remembered which teams each member had played for during their basketball careers. Both Nadine and Gary had pleaded to come to D.C. for this free concert and Nicole had supported their request. Matthew had reluctantly agreed, so here they all were.

It was a beautiful spring day with a slight breeze wafting through the cherry blossoms as the Senator and his family were escorted to the VIP seating of the theater. The cherry blossoms were at "peak bloom" and Nadine waved her cell phone across the expansive crowd, sending video streaming back to her friends in Louisiana.

"Mom, Dad, this is fantastic! Thanks for letting us come!" Nicole and Matthew grinned at each other. It was nice to see her so excited. Even Gary had a continuous grin.

Several people around them recognized Matthew and hollered out to him, "Way to go, Senator! Keep up the good work, Senator."

Matthew waved and smiled, trying to acknowledge each and every one of them. Nicole beamed proudly, while Nadine and Gary were embarrassed.

This is nice, Matthew thought. *Having my family here and being recognized as one of this nation's leaders and heroes.* He continued to smile and wave to the crowd.

As they moved to their seats, another visitor to the concert was working his way towards the center of the crowd. Jonathan Wilson, a/k/a Daib Babar, carried his guitar case over his shoulder as he jostled his way through the crowd. Two hours earlier, Daib and his friends had gathered for special prayers. They had prayed that their missions would cause great panic and death amongst the American infidels: The non-believers who did not deserve to live. The more they prayed, the more their anger grew within them to punish the infidels of America. Following prayers, they had embraced, wished each other well, and departed shouting *Allahu Akbar!* God is Great! They had embraced and left with joy in their hearts. All knew that before the sun set they would be welcomed into heaven as martyrs.

"Excuse me," Daib said politely each time he or his guitar bumped into someone. Inwardly, however, he resented them and knew that soon he would punish them for being part of "the Great Satan."

"That's okay, buddy" the bystanders responded. "Let's all just enjoy the concert."

"You gonna be playin'?" someone asked.

Daib merely smiled and shook his head. *Infidels, I am not here to play. I am here to exact revenge for Islam.* The guitar case was the perfect cover. No one in the crowd expected anything else to be in the case except a guitar. After all, this was to be a concert celebrating the arrival of spring. There would be lots of music and the crowds usually joined in. It was a loud, festive occasion. Daib grinned, but tried to keep his face solemn. *The fools,* he thought, suppressing a grin. *They don't have a clue. They're like cattle waiting to be slaughtered.* Eventually, Daib found a spot on the grass and sat down, clutching his guitar case. He waited patiently for the crowd to "settle in" and for the music to begin. *Infidels, soon you will suffer for your offenses against Allah.*

The concert began and the crowd joined in the singing. Several of the younger observers stood up and swayed to the music. Daib sat quietly, swaying to the music of the first performer while watching the crowd. At the end of the song, the performer bowed, threw kisses to the crowd, and then ran offstage to the noise of raucous applause. As the second performer was being introduced, Daib stood up, and yelled loudly, "*Allahu Akbak!* God is Great!"

Those near him turned to see what the commotion was about. Grinning, Daib pressed the garage door opener in his shirt pocket, sending the required electrical impulse to his bomb detonator. The guitar case exploded, sending thousands of rusty nails and steel balls into the crowd. Daib and seven people near him all died immediately. Many more were injured. The crowd was screaming and running away from the area of the explosion – except for the police who were trying to control the crowd.

"Oh my God!" Nicole screamed. "What was that?" Nadine and Gary were stunned and silent. Matthew sensed trouble.

"Get down!" he screamed, forcing them down. He gathered his family together, trying to cover them with his own body, and then he looked up and saw two men near him with drawn weapons, moving in the direction of the blast yelling to the crowd.

"Make way! FBI!" they shouted.

The Senator recognized the second man. *That's him! That's the guy I saw on the plane! He's a cop!*

Not good, Colossus added.

Tibideaux's mind was racing. His first priority was the protection of his family, but the thought that he was being followed by FBI agents kept screaming into his mind. *What do they want?* he wondered.

Immediately the Theater and the entire National Mall was bedlam. People were running and screaming – most not knowing why- except that everyone around them was screaming – so, they also screamed. Panic is a great motivator, but usually only in causing more panic. The two FBI agents were among the first to reach the point of the explosion.

"FBI," they shouted, flashing their badges. "Please stay calm and move away from the area. Give us some room here." The crowd nearby was trying to escape from the area. The FBI agents cleared the immediate area and then surveyed the damage.

"Damn," the senior agent muttered. "Messy."

The explosion had cut Daib in half. His lower torso was still partially covered by what remained of the guitar. His upper torso had been blown about three feet away. A grin was now frozen permanently on his face. Those victims in the immediate area were bleeding profusely from multiple puncture wounds where they'd been impaled by hundreds of pieces of metal. Uniformed police and other first responders arrived almost immediately after the FBI agents. The scene was gruesome. The seven dead had all been closest to Daib. All had died from head wounds as the nails entered their eyes and temples.

"Oh my God!" Nicole screamed. "What's happening?"

"Just stay down," Matthew ordered. He held them all down below the seats until he heard the sound of sirens arriving. The crowd was still in a state of panic. Matthew waited until the police had circled the amphitheater and then instructed his family, "Okay. Get up slowly and follow me," he said.

"What is it, Dad?" Both children were asking.

"I don't know. Sounded like a bomb or something. Best thing we can do is to leave here quickly," he replied as he led them back to their car. The metropolitan police had arrived and cordoned off all of the parking areas. They stopped each vehicle and required the occupants to provide identification. Some cars were pulled over and searched. Moving through the checkpoints, the traffic was painfully slow. They didn't get back to the apartment until nearly dark.

Exploding into the apartment, Gary grabbed the remote and found a local TV station. The news was on every channel.

"BREAKING NEWS!! BREAKING NEWS!!" flashed continuously across the bottom of the screen.

"A series of terrible tragedies has occurred here in the capitol," a reporter announced, sadly shaking his head. "Today, three Islamic terrorist suicide bombers detonated homemade bombs in the Metropolitan area, at three separate metro locations. The first detonation occurred in the midst of the crowd during the Cherry Blossom Festival Concert at the base of the Washington Monument. Initial reports indicate at least eight people are dead, including the bomber. Unconfirmed reports are that an additional twenty people have been taken to local hospitals. There are no confirmed reports as to the extent of their injuries, but we here at the Capitol's finest news station will keep you abreast of any and all developments. We go now to the site of the concert bombing where our field reporter, John Wayne, is speaking with authorities. Are you there, John?"

"Yes, Bill. I'm here on site and the Chief of Police is about to speak."

The camera cut away to the Chief of Police, standing at a makeshift podium. "Thank you." The Chief began. "I have a short statement. I will not answer any questions until we can investigate this incident further. What we do know is that a young man in his early 20's detonated a homemade bomb here in the National Mall at approximately 3:15 p.m. Witnesses say that just before he detonated the bomb, he shouted *'Allahu Akbar*. God is Great.' Eight people died in the blast, including the bomber. Except for the bomber himself, the deaths do not appear to be from the explosive device itself, rather they resulted from the shrapnel in the form of nails and steel balls packed tightly around the explosive. A number of other bystanders were injured and have been taken to hospitals. We will make a more definitive statement later this evening. Thank you." A gaggle of reporters waved their hands for attention and shouted out questions. The Chief ignored them and continued the investigation.

"Back to you, Bill."

"Thanks, John. As we said previously, there were a total of three detonations. The second bomb was detonated at the Amtrak Union Station and the third was at the Montgomery Mall in Bethesda, Maryland. We're receiving sketchy reports from both locations, but initially it appears that one bomber passed through the grand waiting room. We have some video from security cameras showing him walking and carrying a backpack as he entered the train platform." Across the screen came a streaming video of a young man with a backpack walking nonchalantly towards the trains. "He then boarded an eastbound local and detonated the bomb as the train pulled out of the station. The car was derailed. Preliminary reports indicate three dead and at least twelve injured. Amtrak has cancelled all trains both into and out of the Washington Union Station until further notice.

"Finally, in Bethesda, a bomb was detonated in the large food court area of the Montgomery Mall. At least seven are known dead and the number of injured is still to be determined. All three bombs were detonated within fifteen minutes of each other. All three bombs appear to have been similar in design. The police have also made some preliminary identification on the three suicide bombers. Although names are being withheld until further investigations have been conducted, it appears that two of the three bombers are American citizens, born and raised here in the U.S. The third bomber is believed to be a Palestinian who appears to have entered the U.S. by crossing the U.S. - Mexican border. There you have it,

Washington. The response here in the metropolitan area has been extensive. We have reports of several Muslims and mosques being attacked by angry citizens. For more on this we go now to Mary Fortnite at the Georgetown Mosque."

"Hi, Bill," the reporter began. "I am speaking with the conservative Imam, Ahmed Ramadi. He deplores the most recent suicide bomb attacks. Mr. Ramadi."

"Yes," the Imam began. "These people are not true followers of Islam. They are extremists who are violating the laws of Islam. The Quran specifically forbids suicide attacks. To do so is to pervert the teachings of Islam. America needs to realize that the vast majority of Muslims wish to live in peace. We in the Muslim community deplore these attacks and we grieve for the victims. Please do not hate all of us for the actions of the few."

"Right," Gary yelled. "Nobody else is killing Americans except you damn Muslims. We oughta blow your asses away!"

"Gary," Nicole cautioned. "That's no way to talk."

"But Mom," he pleaded, "it's the truth. Look at how many times they've attacked us and our government just lets them get away with it. Are we afraid of them or something?"

"I know, I know," she whispered.

"Then we should do something," Gary argued.

"I know, Sweetheart, and I agree, but that's for the law to handle."

"But nobody does anything, Mom."

Tibideaux watched the program intently, but his mind was elsewhere. *Who were those two men? Why were they following me?*

The two FBI agents gave their reports to the police and then phoned in their reports to FBI headquarters. Included in their FBI report was that they had lost the Senator in the excitement;

however, they were en route to his apartment, since the GPS indicated his vehicle was parked at home.

"Told ya," the elder agent said to the group standing around the office coffee machine.

"Told us what?" someone asked.

"That pulling agents off of the jihad operation to check out some damn Senator was a mistake. Remember? I told ya that we were gonna get spread so thin that one of these bastards would slip through. How many dead?"

"Eighteen, at last count," someone replied.

"Well, I hope the brass realizes their mistake here. Don't be surprised if we get a few more bombers being successful in a very short time. This is a goddamn war, yet the politicians won't admit it. It's not the politically correct thing to do."

"Yeah," someone offered. "How many of us have to die before the assholes running the country figure it out? Most of them are afraid to say the words 'Jihad Terrorist.' Maybe we ought to tattoo those words on their fucking foreheads."

"Hey guys, check out Channel 3." An agent at Headquarters yelled into the break room. "Al Qaeda is claiming responsibility for the bomb at the Washington Monument."

The entire group leaned forward to hear the actual report. A senior member of Al Qaeda warned that there would be more attacks in the near future. He indicated that this attack was part of a larger, coordinated effort.

"No way," the elder agent responded. "These explosives were amateurish... deadly, but amateurish. Al Qaeda had nothing to do with this."

"Maybe so," another agent responded. "But, they've been saying they were going to step up the attacks on us."

"Yeah, we're gonna have our hands full. Somehow, they're getting more and more of our own kids turning against us. I don't understand it."

"Well," someone else offered, "most of us are fed up with all the crooked politicians and when we go home we don't talk about the good things Americans do. Most of us complain. I think that's part of it." Heads nodded in agreement.

The Chinese Embassy issued a statement of condolence to the families of the victims. China denounced the bombers and offered whatever assistance Washington might need. The world applauded their humanitarian offer.

Sixteen

"Economics Are Trump"

Nicole and the children returned to New Orleans Monday morning. Matthew returned to the Senate for the most hectic week of his career. It was also a hectic time for the country and for the government. The administration had continued to spend excessively and to increase the national debt. Both China and Russia announced publicly that they favored a new International Reserve Currency which immediately sent the value of the dollar into a tailspin. Gold and silver made amazing leaps in value, as did most commodities. Gasoline prices at the pump had gone to over six dollars a gallon. The mood of the nation was "gnarly" at best.

"The American debt structure," said the Russian President at a world economic summit meeting, "places the world in a precarious position. The world can no longer afford to have the world reserve currency be the currency of the greatest debtor nation in the history of the world. The Russian Government will press for the euro to replace the U.S. dollar as the world's reserve currency."

Several of the Shia governments in the Middle East agreed. With each pronouncement, the value of the dollar went down and the price of gas went up. The Chinese announced that they would be amenable to having the Yuan become the International Reserve Currency if that would help stabilize the world financial crisis. These actions and the bombs in the capitol, followed by additional Al Qaeda threats, drove the stock market down over 500 points the following week. Anger and frustration seethed through the population. Debate in Congress was vitriolic. Each side of the aisle blamed the other side for the growing economic crisis. The President formed a Special Council and the council recommended a reduction in funds for all discretionary programs, including the contract Tibideaux had promised Yao. Tibideaux was furious and began to lobby for an exception. He did not tell Yao of the setback. The EPA also announced that once again it would be reviewing the ban on drilling in the Gulf. No action would be taken, pending the review.

"What?" Tibideaux screamed when informed. "I have promised jobs to my constituents."

He called the administrator of the EPA. He'd worked far too hard to get these wells back in operation. His reputation as "the People's Senator" was riding on his providing jobs for Louisiana and the Gulf States. "Who authorized these delays?" he demanded to know.

"I'm sorry, Senator," the Director of the EPA replied. "Our hands are tied here. There's nothing I can do until this crisis abates," the administrator confessed. "We know there's a need in your state, but we just don't have the money. We must reduce the debt and we cannot afford to have another debacle like the BP oil spill. So even though we could use the income from the oil, we just cannot afford to risk another big expense and to once again disrupt the economics of the Gulf Coast."

Tibideaux was furious. He scheduled an appointment with the Senate Majority Leader.

"Good afternoon, Senator," the Majority Leader welcomed him. "What can I do for the Senator from Louisiana, today?"

"Well, I understand that the funds we discussed for Louisiana have been scuttled, is that true?"

"Yes, unfortunately, we're all having to make some sacrifices under the current conditions. As soon as all of this clears up, and the economy gets back on track, you will still get the money. This is just a short delay."

"But I need this contract now," Tibideaux pleaded. "I've made promises."

"Yes, well, haven't we all?" the Leader replied. "This is the nature of the game, Matthew. Sometimes we have to step back, take a hit, and then prepare to move on."

"So," Matthew asked. "When do you think we can get things moving again? My people need these jobs."

"I understand," said the Speaker, slowly tilting his chair towards the desk. "And I'm deeply moved over the compassion you have for your constituents. We need more men like you in Congress – people who are committed to the American people, you know, all those little people out there. I congratulate you and I promise you that we will prevail. We just need to slow down a bit until life settles down, okay?"

Dejected, Matthew returned to his apartment. *How am I going to tell my constituents? And Yao? Bezzos will crucify me for breaking my promise to the people.* Matthew didn't know what to do. He didn't know what he feared most – the response from his constituents... or Bezzos... or Yao. None of his prospects excited him.

As he sat in his apartment considering possible courses of action, Colossus spoke up. *Sometimes, a little action can clear the head. You need something to help you think more clearly and that something is action. Time to punish some of the guilty.*

"But who?" Matthew asked in reply.

Let's go look, Colossus whispered. *Remember when we first decided to strike the MS-13? We knew that they were enemies.*

Remember how good it felt to be on the front lines of America? Well, now we know. MS-13 has helped smuggle in illegals. They're probably responsible for bringing in that Palestinian who blew up Union Station. I say we seek revenge for America, but we must be very careful. They'll be expecting something and they'll be ready. Tibideaux agreed.

"Hey, look," Special Agent Jones grabbed his partner's arm. "He's taking a cab. Follow him."

Tibideaux's cab drove past the sedan with the two agents. Tibideaux noticed the sedan had two occupants – both men. He disregarded it, busy with designing his plan for the next hit.

The agents followed him to the airport and watched him pay for the cab ride, then board a rental car shuttle bus.

"What the hell is he doing?" one asked.

"Maybe he's got a date or something." They followed his rental car back to his apartment, where the Senator parked the rental car in front of the house and then went inside.

"This is crazy," Agent Andy Micah whispered.

Shortly after midnight, the Senator came out of the house, smeared something over the license plate, and then got into the rental car.

"That looks like a rifle he's carrying!" Micah blurted out. "And what is that shit he put on the license plate?"

"Don't know, follow him." Jones ordered.

"Don't you think we'd better stop him?"

"For what? Not tipping the cabbie? Or for wiping his hands on the plate?"

"No, the rifle."

"No law against that. We could ask for his permit and blow our cover. No, let's just keep an eye on him."

"Okay."

Tibideaux drove aimlessly around the city for over an hour, but couldn't identify a worthy target. *Go to the International Corridor*, Colossus suggested. Tibideaux complied. Arriving at the Tokoma/Langley crossroads, Tibideaux realized that he had been followed by the same car for some time. He drove through the area, making a few turns, and then waited for the suspicious vehicle. Twice he drove past groups that were obviously MS-13. As he drove by, each group stopped their chatter and guardedly watched as he cruised by.

They're ready for a fight, Colossus observed, *but this is not the right time. They aren't the right target. Let's keep looking.*

"Not tonight," Matthew said, heading back to his apartment. "Something doesn't feel right." He wouldn't let Colossus reply.

"What the hell is he doing?" asked the lead agent.

"Don't know. Think he made us?" his partner asked.

"Don't know. None of this makes any sense to me. Why the cab? Why the rental? Why the rifle? Why this late at night?"

"And why this part of town?" Jones added.

Tibideaux headed back towards the center of the city, then pulled into a deserted drive and cut his lights. The driveway was largely covered by overgrown Azalea bushes and hid the car from the street.

"Damn," Micah exclaimed. I think he made us and then pulled a fast one. I lost him at that last light."

They drove around the area awhile longer, unable to regain contact. Finally they returned to their spot across from the Senator's apartment, all the while cursing the fact that a politician had given them the slip. It was embarrassing to them both.

Meanwhile, Tibideaux waited in the dark until he felt the car following him was gone. He returned to the International Corridor and found a group still loitering on a corner. They all turned and watched as he drove past. Tibideaux turned the corner, pulling only a few yards down the street.

Following his now standard M.O. he moved quietly back to the corner, peering around to view the target group. They were engrossed in their loud conversation so he prepared himself for action. He leaned into the building for support, identified two targets, and slowly brought the rifle up into a firing position. He took aim on his first target and had begun to draw in his long, slow breath when one of the gang members yelled something. A slight movement of his rifle had caught a glint from the streetlight and the gang member had seen it. He alerted the gang and they turned just as Tibideaux pulled the trigger.

Whut! The initial target dropped to the ground, but this time the gang was ready. They all fired in his direction. Multiple rounds flew around and past him. One bullet struck the corner of the building, sending a piece of broken concrete into his right cheek, just below his eye. He felt a sharp pain, but remained focused. Simultaneously, they began running towards him, firing. Sections of the building's corner flew off in all directions as the gang's fire bit into the building.

Matthew fired off three quick rounds; dropping two of the gang members. When they fell, the others dove for cover, still firing, but no longer advancing. Their delay gave Tibideaux time to make his escape. Down the dark street, into his car, and off into the night he fled. They didn't follow. He returned home, parked the car, and went inside.

"He's back." The lead agent woke his sleeping partner. "Mark the time."

Damn, Colossus laughed. *Now, that was exciting! And, I think you got more than one!* Tibideaux grimaced slightly, *Yeah,* he thought, *but how bad was I hit?* He went into the bathroom and examined his cheek. It wasn't as bad as he first thought, but it would probably leave a scar... *and it'll be swollen in the morning.* He cleaned out the wound and applied ice to keep the swelling down. *I don't want to do this anymore,* he informed Colossus. *This was too close. That's it.* Colossus did not argue. *Tomorrow, with a clear head we can re-evaluate,* he whispered.

The following morning Tibideaux returned the rental car and took a cab back to his apartment. He was aware of the two men who followed him. *Who are they?* he wondered. *They were armed – probably police or even FBI. But why are they following me?*

The FBI agents were equally puzzled. "Okay," Andy Micah mused. He takes a ride, but not in his own car. Whatever he's doing, he really wants to cover his tracks. What could it be?

"Well," his partner replied, "at first, I thought he was going to meet some broad, but when he came out with the rifle, hell, that blew my theory all to hell. Think we ought to try and get a warrant? You know – check out the place?"

"Naw," Andy replied. "We need one helluva lot more info to get a warrant on a Senator. Let's just keep a closer watch."

"One thing's for sure," Jones laughed. "The way he changes vehicles, the department couldn't afford enough GPS trackers."

That morning, the TV announcers excitedly reported on the night's activities.

"Good Morning, America. Last night Washington was a reprise for the Old West. Possibly a return to the "shootout at the OK corral." Early this morning, a shooter, or shooters attempted to engage a local gang in a massive shootout on the International

Corridor area. Three youths were killed and another wounded. The shooter, or shooters, managed to escape. Authorities have informed us that the rounds found in the victims are identical to those of the three other shootings earlier this year. This is, however, the first time that shell casings have been found. Evidently, the gang was at least partially prepared and did not allow the shooter enough time to pick up his expended brass. The police are convinced that all four crimes are related. If you have information relevant to these shootings, please call CRIMESTOPPERS."

Matthew Tibideaux was too excited to go to his office. Instead, he called Yao. He knew that Yao would be upset and from somewhere in his memory, Tibideaux remembered an old saying that 'one should always deliver bad news quickly'. *Yao is a business man,* he thought. *By keeping him informed early, he should appreciate that it is not my fault and that we will still get the contract. This is only a minor delay.*

Sue Guifei answered the phone. "Good morning, Future Technologies, Sue Guifei speaking."

"Good morning, Ms Guifei," the Senator replied. May I speak with Mr. Yao?"

"He is away at a business meeting. May I be of assistance?"

"When will he be back?" Tibideaux asked.

"Some time tomorrow, I believe. What can I do to help?"

"Just have him call me when he returns. There appears to be a change in our plans."

"Oh? Is anything wrong? she asked.

"No, I just need to talk with him. Thanks."

Sue Guifei immediately called Fred Ming Yao, who was meeting with his Intelligence handler. "There appears to be a problem with our senator," she said.

"I'll call you right back," Yao replied.

"And so," Yao's handler continued, "your country wants you to pursue our venture with added haste. If we, along with Russia, succeed in removing the United States dollar as the world's reserve currency, the economic plunge of America could be much more rapid and severe than we had originally expected. If so, we may wish to act more quickly in pushing for their collapse. If we can have The Golden Dragon in place before that occurs, we will have a superb advantage. We could dominate them by the mere threat of force. We could bring them to their knees without ever risking the life of a single Chinese soldier."

"I will do what I can," Yao promised solemnly.

"Listen to this." FBI Agent Micah tapped Agent Jones on the shoulder and turned up the radio. The announcer was repeating the information from the previous night's shootings.

"Holy crap!" Jones exclaimed. "The International Corridor – last night, shortly after midnight!"

"That's the time and general location when we lost the senator. We know he was carrying a rifle!" You don't think there could be a connection, do you?"

"Well, that's one helluva lot of 'circumstantial' to get started on," Jones responded. "We need to get to headquarters and possibly coordinate with the local police. Let's go!"

"But what about the senator? Shouldn't we keep an eye on him here?"

"You're right. You stay here, I'll call for a ride. There's gotta be a metro cop nearby. I'll go to HQ and start the action. Call if you need any backup."

"Got it."

Agent Jones was picked up by a local patrol car and taken to FBI Headquarters. En route, he called in to the duty desk to start gathering the necessary people to discuss a course of action.

Meanwhile, at the Metro police headquarters, detectives Gutierrez and Rounds were excitedly discussing the latest shootings.

"He's getting sloppy," Rounds announced. "He left shell casings behind."

"Yeah, but there were no fingerprints," Gutierrez replied. "Looks like he wore gloves as he loaded up, maybe even when he's poppin' caps, So, I'd say he's still pretty cagey."

"You're right, but..." Rounds added. "In his prep, he's still cool, but maybe, just maybe he's gettin' a bit cocky. He had to know after that last MS-13 shooting that these guys would be ready for a fight *next* time. Like I said, *last time*. Killin' homeless guys is one thing, but takin' on MS-13 is a horse of a different color."

"You said that?" Gutierrez asked with a grin. "I thought I was the one who made that observation!"

"Well," laughed Rounds. "One of us was smart enough to think it, so who really cares which one? We're a team, right?" They both laughed and gave each other a knuckle dap. They were interrupted by another detective calling to them.

"Hey, if you two jokesters are through fartin' around here, there's some guy from the FBI who wants to talk to you. Says it's about the shooting last night. Line two."

"Gutierrez here," said the lead detective.

"Jones here, FBI. Is there a chance we could talk? I think I might have something on last night's shooting. It involves a case we're working on. My partner and I think we may have a connection."

"Sure! Where and when?" Gutierrez was interested.

"Why don't we come downtown to your office? Say 10 a.m.?"

The detective glanced up at the wall clock – 8:30. "Yeah, sounds good. See you then."

"Roger," Jones replied and hung up.

Seventeen

"Reap the Rewards of Corruption"

Joe Scorso paced back and forth across his living room floor.

"What's the matter, Joe?" his wife asked, concerned at his behavior.

"Nothin'," he replied. "Just got a lot on my mind. Need to sort some stuff out."

"Like what?" she asked.

"Remember when I told you about that senator – the one I think is crooked?"

"Yes."

"Well, I think he's involved with some really bad shit, stuff that could really be dangerous for all of us here in the U.S. I told those guys in Louisiana and that one guy said he was gonna report it to the FBI. He said he did, but now I don't know what to do. Remember how my dad used to talk about all those posters and slogans in World War Two, how the government wanted everybody to help keep the country strong? You know, report suspicious stuff?"

"Yeah," she answered. "And some folks made fun of him."

"Right. Well now it's my turn. Maybe the Senator doesn't realize what he's doing. I gotta give him a chance. I'm gonna call him."

"Wait a minute. If it's as bad as you think, do you really want to get involved?" His wife's eyes had a troubled look.

"Well, I've reported it to the authorities. Last week, I did some snoopin' and I got his phone number. I think it's his cell. Got it from some papers on Guifei's desk. He won't even know who called him. I'm gonna call from a pay phone in another part of town. Whaddya think?"

"Well, I think you should call that first guy you spoke with — Spade...or somethin' like that. Don't think I could handle you getting deeply involved in this kinda mess."

"Maybe you're right, but this is kinda like stopping the enemy from sinking a ship or something."

"Fine," she shot back. "What does this have to do with ships?"

"Nothin'... just another poster reference."

Joe got into his car. A few minutes later he pulled into a downtown gas station and walked over to the public phone next to the air machine. Reaching into his jacket pocket, he found the piece of paper he wanted, picked up the phone, and dialed the Senator's cell phone.

Tibideaux was headed to the Washington office of Future Technologies, Inc. to pick up another "package" when his cell phone rang. He hadn't told Yao that the contract would not be forthcoming. The ringing of the phone irritated him. He had important things on his mind. "Yes, Senator Tibideaux here," he said and then waited for a response.

"Yao is a spy for China," the voice said. "And you're a traitor."

Click. The caller hung up before the senator could reply.

Who was that? he wondered. *And how did they get my private number? Yao, a spy? What the hell is going on?* The senator didn't mind making a few bucks here and there, but working with a spy? That would be treason. He was a patriot, not a spy! He was not a traitor! He was one of the leaders of the country. He would get to the bottom of this right now.

A short time later, he walked into the office of the Executive Vice President of Operations, Future Technologies, Inc.

Agent Jones followed him and watched him enter the offices of Future Technologies. He then called his partner, Micah, who was entering the Metro Police Department headquarters.

"Okay," Jones reported, "he's entered the main offices of that Chinese outfit he's supposed to be working with. What do I do now?"

"You wait. I'm just now getting in to talk to the detectives on the shooting cases. Stay in touch. I think this could be a big day for all of us."

"Welcome, Senator," Sue Guifei smiled pleasantly as the Senator entered her office. "Are you here for your package?"

"Hello, Ms. Guifei, Matthew replied. "Perhaps, but first I need some information. What other operations are you running here?"

"Why? What do you mean?" she asked softly.

"I just got a phone call, a man who said that this is a spy operation!"

"Really? How ridiculous! Who was this call from? Are they competitors who would like to shut us down? Are they someone who is jealous of our success? Who made this call?"

"I don't know," the Senator replied.

"You don't know?" Sue Guifei's eyebrows arched. "You come here and insult me based on a phone call from someone you don't know?"

"I know, it sounds silly, but there's been so much happening lately."

"You've been with us for a long time. Do we look like spies?" Ms. Guifei asked sharply.

"Just answer the question!" the Senator responded, growing irritated.

"No! We are not spies. We are just business people... just like you." She retorted.

"I'm not like you," Matthew shouted, nervously fiddling with his coat buttons.

"No?" she challenged. She approached him and stroked his hair, trying to tone him down, while avoiding his questions.

"No," he said, brushing her hand away.

"Well," she purred, "all this time we've been good friends. Haven't we always paid you as we promised?"

"Yes," he replied, "but maybe I didn't understand everything."

"Oh, come now," she chided. "You're an intelligent man. It appears you know how to conduct a business venture, do you not?" She smiled.

"That's beside the point!" he argued. "I thought this was strictly a commercial venture – an attempt to help the people of my state."

"Even so," she continued, obviously trying to seduce him. "What about the women? You enjoyed them, didn't you?" She touched his arm with the envelope.

"I don't want your money," he responded, pushing the envelope away. "Yes, I enjoyed the women, but that was before. Now I want some answers."

"I don't understand. We've given you what... about two hundred thousand dollars? "Won't it help with your campaigns? Regardless of whether you run for Senator again or run for Governor, it will help you. Through our programs, you have added jobs and pleased your people. It's only right that you should also be pleased – and have pleasure, is it not?"

"Yes, yes... but I thought that was just business."

"And it was, just as this package is."

"I told you, I don't want that money. I just want answers. I want to talk with Yao."

"And I told you, it was business, just like the other money we gave you to help us get contracts, nothing more. Mr. Yao is not available at this time. I will give him your message."

"And how do I know that?"

"I guess you'll just have to trust us as we have trusted you," she whispered, moving closer and placing one hand on his thigh. Her other hand, still holding the "package" rested on his shoulder. "There's no reason for you to be upset. We are not spies. You know," she said, shifting her body slightly towards him. She touched the gauze patch on his cheek. "What happened here? Does it hurt? Maybe I could make it better for you?"

He brushed her hand away. "Just a scratch, it's okay."

"I have often wished that it was I with whom you celebrated after our dinners. I think you would have liked that too, wouldn't you?" She moved her hand further up his thigh, rubbing firmly against his growing erection. He sucked in a deep breath.

"Would you like to have me – right here and now?" she asked, caressing his manhood.

"No, not now," he protested, raising his hands in front of him, but allowing her to continue. He knew this was wrong, but the thought of having sex with this beautiful, sensual woman was almost overwhelming.

She leaned over and kissed him on the neck while pulling on his zipper to open his trousers. He pushed her hand away and stepped back.

"No!" he said firmly. "Nothing more until I get some answers. Have Yao call me. I need answers before we do any more business."

The senator stood up, brushed past Ms. Guifei, and walked out the door.

She watched him with a quizzical, disappointed look on her face and then she called Yao. "We have a problem," she said.

"Oh?"

"The senator just left here after accusing us of being spies. What should we do?"

"Be patient for now. Were the security systems in operation?"

"Yes," she replied.

"Good. First, we try to reason with him."

"That will not work," she interrupted. "I tried, but he's like a dog with rabies."

"I see. Well then, we must threaten him with exposure. He must be kept silent about our ventures."

"And if that does not work?" she asked.

"Then Gunter will have to dispose of him. But first call him and inform him that we have proof of his accepting our 'packages' and that we will expose him, if necessary. Then make travel arrangements for you and me. If we must take action – either to expose him – or kill him, we must be out of this country before we do so or we will spend many years in an American jail. That is *not* something I wish to do."

Meanwhile, Tibideaux had gotten into his car and headed for the Senate. He didn't notice the car following him. His mind was racing over the recent events.

His cell phone rang again. He answered angrily. "What?" he shouted.

"Senator?" It was Sue Guifei.

"I told you, I don't want to talk to you until you're ready to give me answers. Have Yao call me."

"Yes, I will, but before you hang up, I must inform you that my office security cameras were in excellent operating condition while you and I were having our little talk about the money and women you have received from us. Now that you have 'gotten religion'... I think that's the American saying, would you like a copy sent to your home or to the FBI... or perhaps both?"

Click. She'd hung up.

The senator tried to call her back. There was no answer. He tried to call Yao. There was no answer.

Meanwhile, at police headquarters, the homicide detectives and the FBI agent were comparing notes.

"Okay," Detective Bosco asked, "So, you guys saw him with the rifle, and acting kinda weird. You then followed him into the general area of the crime scene. Just after midnight, you lost him. Then, you saw him come home around four in the morning."

"That's right."

"So, he had the opportunity. He was in the area. And, he had a weapon that could fit the murder weapon."

"That's right."

"Anything else?"

"No," Special Agent Jones replied. "He's a weird duck. We're following him on a possible lead that he's selling national security secrets to some damn Chinese spy. So it seems like he's possibly involved in all kinds of illegal activity."

"Think we have enough for a search warrant?" asked the detective.

"Yeah, I think we do – at least enough for an ordinary citizen, but I don't know about a politician, especially a U.S. Senator. Not many judges will risk offending that kind of power."

"So what do we do now?"

"Excuse me." A member of the investigating team entered the room.

"Yeah, what's up?" Detective Bosco asked.

"Thought you might like to know. We've matched all of the rounds used in these murders. They're all from the same weapon. The rounds indicate it was a 30.06. So it's the same guy in every killing and only one shooter. This guy's a loner."

"Great, thanks," Gutierrez said.

"Yeah, Jones replied. "Good work. Okay, can you hold off on that search warrant for a couple more hours? I want to check the records and see if our Senator was in the D.C. area on the night of the other three shootings."

"Can do," Gutierrez replied. "If you get some confirmation, we tell the chief, and let him work the local politics... and then we wait."

Jones called the Bureau and talked to the researchers on duty. "Find out everything you can about the whereabouts of Senator Matthew Tibideaux on the following dates." He gave them the dates of the shootings. "I especially want to know if he has any alibis for those nights. This is a real rush job. Top Priority!"

"Got it." Jones called his partner. "What's happening?"

"Nothin'. He left that Chinese office and came straight home. Been in there ever since. Did you get anything?"

"Yeah, a lot. I'm having the Bureau check out his whereabouts on the nights of all the killings. He could be the serial killer."

"Damn... and a traitor, too!" The agent whistled softly. "I hope we can wrap this up quickly. Can you imagine how the shit will hit the fan if this is true and the news media gets hold of it before we wrap it up?"

"Yeah, I do. It won't be pretty. Okay, soon as I hear anything, I'll give you a call."

It was the following morning before the staff got back to Jones. "Well," the researcher began, "I didn't get to check on any people with possible alibis, but I did find that he was in D.C. every night and his social calendar was clean."

"Thanks." Jones called Bosco. They agreed to meet immediately.

"So what did you find out?" Bosco asked.

"The bastard was here every single time there was a killing."

"No kidding?"

"Scout's honor." Jones held his hand up in the Boy Scout salute.

"Okay, I'll talk to the Chief." Gutierrez arranged to meet with the Chief of Police for Washington, D.C. A few hours later, he returned.

"The Chief is talking to some judges, trying to get a warrant. He says to hold tight. It'll probably be tomorrow before he can get one to let it all hang out enough to put a warrant on a U.S. Senator. So in the meantime, we wait."

"Okay," said Jones. "In the meantime, I gotta get back to my partner. We'll continue our surveillance. Keep me posted, okay?"

"Absolutely. Nice working with you."

Eighteen

"When the Chickens Come Home to Roost"

Matthew didn't sleep for two days following his meeting with Sue Guifei. He did take frequent showers and scrubbed his body hard in the places where she'd touched him. *What am I gonna do?* he asked himself over and over.

Finally, Colossus spoke to him. *You are now the guilty one. You know you must be punished. You know what we must do.*

"Well," Tibideaux shouted, "I am going to get to the bottom of this!"

You are the bottom, Colossus whispered in his ear. *It's time for you to do your duty. You are a disgrace to yourself, to the Senate, and to your country. That is why those FBI men have been following you. They know. It is only a matter of time.*

"But what about my family?"

You should have thought about that earlier, Colossus scolded him. *And, now you must show the courage of a leader. It is time to do your duty.*

"What do you mean?" Matthew asked. "What duty?"

You know what I mean, Colossus responded.

Tibideaux opened the closet and grabbed the rifle. He entered the bedroom. Tears were flowing freely down his cheeks. He knew what Colossus meant and he knew it would be final.

The following morning, the FBI and the Metropolitan police approached Tibideaux's apartment in a tactical formation. Jones and Bosco were in the lead. Rounds knocked on the door. "Senator Tibideaux!" she shouted. "This is the police and the FBI. We have a warrant to search the premises."

There was no reply. The SWAT team spread out for security. Micah and Jones kicked the door in and entered with weapons drawn. "FBI!" they shouted and began to clear the rooms.

"In here!" Jones called out.

On the floor of the bedroom lay the body of the Senator. He'd placed the muzzle of the rifle well into his mouth. The back of his head was sprayed over the bedroom wall and what remained was only a gaping hole. The gauze bandage on his cheek remained.

The following morning, "Spud" placed a call to Sam in Louisiana. Hey," he shouted into the phone. "Front page of the *Washington Post*. Senator Matthew Tibideaux of Louisiana found dead of an apparent suicide. The cops found him this morning. Just thought you ought to know."

"Holy shit!" Sam muttered. "How did it happen?"

"Story says he put a rifle barrel in his mouth and BAM! Took the big bite!"

"Do you think it was related to the Chinese?"

"Don't know," Spud replied. "But, if you want, I'll do some checking. Think there might be some more of those politicians involved?"

"You never know. Yeah, see what you can find out. I'm going in to my boss right now and bring him up to speed. This could get nasty."

"Hey," Spud asked. "Was this guy a Republican or a Democrat?"

"What difference does it make?" Sam asked. "They're all crooked. Doesn't make a damn what party."

Sam turned off his phone and headed towards his headquarters. He really hoped this was an isolated event, but like most Americans, he'd learned over the past few years that it was a serious mistake to ever trust any American politician, regardless of their party affiliation. He didn't trust any of them.

The FBI arrested Yao and Guifei on charges of espionage and closed down their operation. Without the contract from Tibideaux, the Chinese weren't able to infect the American Missile Defense System—or any other system.

America didn't know that on this night we could put our children to bed with greater confidence.

The investigation of the Senator's suicide resulted in a matching of the bullets used in the earlier shootings in the city. A high-level committee was formed to conduct the full investigation. At the conclusion, the committee was certain that all of the shootings were related, but were reluctant to allow this information to be made public. The random shootings were classified as "unsolved" and relegated to the "cold case" files. The Senator's death was proclaimed to be a self-inflicted fatal wound performed as a result of stress over the loss of the potential employment opportunities for his constituents. At his funeral, there were many poignant speeches given recounting his many virtues and proclaiming his death to be a great loss for America.

A gag order was imposed on both the FBI investigators and the D.C. Metro detectives. The authorities didn't want to tarnish the senator's reputation – or to cause a national panic over security. His death was officially proclaimed to be a suicide due to stress.

"I'm gonna fight this gag order." Rounds was furious. "He's a goddamn spy. Why should we protect his reputation?"

"Look," Gutierrez cautioned, "I'm with you on this, but this gag order came from really high up. No way in hell we could win. Best we can do is shut up and then ten years from now spill the beans in our memoirs. Raise a stink now and you'll not only lose your job, you'll be blacklisted in every place in the country."

"No shit?" Rounds asked.

"No shit."

Rounds kicked the desk and left the building. "No wonder our country is no longer respected around the world," she muttered.

A group of Senators and Congressmen demanded an investigation into why the FBI had failed to prevent the bombings in the nation's capitol, with threats of "cleaning house" on the agency for failing to protect the American people. It was all talk – all for show with no real action intended, merely political posturing. Several American judges issued statements that under certain circumstances Muslims living in America were *not* required to live by American laws; if they wished, they were allowed to live under Sharia law. After all, Americans are a generous and giving people.

Nineteen

"The Aftermath"

Immediately after hearing the news, members of Tibideaux's staff had gone to the senator's home to console and to be of assistance to his family. They answered all of the phone calls, arranged for meals for the family, and received the many friends and neighbors who came to express their condolences.

"The family is holding up about as well as can be expected," they told friends and the media. "This is all such a shock. The family is grateful for your thoughts and prayers. Yes, we will tell them they are in your prayers. Thank you for coming by."

Why? Nicole asked herself. *Was there something that I did? I thought he loved us. I thought he was happy. To kill himself, he could not have loved us as much as I thought. Why?* Falling into the porch lounger, her body racked with pain, she couldn't stop asking the same question. *Why?*

Nadine was hysterical. Two members of the staff were constantly at her side.

"Why did he do this?" she yelled at the staff members. "Why?"

"No one knows," they would reply. "Seems he was stressed out over the cutbacks and he knew the hardships this would cause the people of Louisiana. He was that kind of man."

"Oh, yeah?" Nadine screamed. "How 'bout the hardships for his family? Didn't he care about us? Were they more important to him than his family? We loved him long before he ever went into politics. I guess he didn't love us, at least not as much as he loved his damn constituents."

"Come, now, Nadine. You don't mean that. Your daddy loved you. You know he did. Everybody knows that."

"No, I don't... and don't you try to tell me he did. If he did, he'd be here with us instead of in some damn morgue in Washington." The staffers knew this was a battle they couldn't win, so they wrapped their arms around her, held her, and let her cry.

Gary locked himself in his room, bewildered. He didn't speak to anyone. He merely sat silently on his bed, fighting the pain, as the tears washed down his face.

Across town, Johnny and Melinda sat, bewildered, in their kitchen.

"What the hell?" Johnny asked. "This doesn't make any sense at all. Hell, he was riding high. What happened? There has got to be more to the story than what we're hearing. A guy riding this high doesn't just go and whack himself."

"And his family," Melinda added. "My heart aches for them. This has got to be brutal to live through. I don't know if I'd want to go on if I lost you, especially so early in life."

Johnny walked across the room, wrapped his arms around her, and pulled her close. "Yeah, I feel the same. Wouldn't want to go through my life without you." He rested his chin on the top of her head. "But I'm sure they'll make it. Nicole is a tough woman. It's the kids I feel most for. The daughter worshipped her dad. This has gotta be tearin' her apart. Should we call, or go over, or something?"

"We should wait," Melinda said. "Right now, they mostly need family and close friends. Let's give them some respect and some space. We can go over later, once this has all calmed down a bit. But it kinda settles it for me. I don't want you to run for senator."

"I've been thinkin' along the same lines, Honey. I'm certain that there is more here than meets the eye and I really don't want any part of it. I'm not running."

Twenty

"Once More: Beijing"

"Mr. Chairman." The three Vice-Chairmen of the Chinese Central Military Commission addressed their leader, Li Hung-Tsao.

"Yes, Gentlemen. What is your purpose for this meeting?" The Chairman sat erect in his chair, impeccable in his Mao jacket, his glasses framing his wide eyes.

The three men, all generals in the People's Liberation Army and well-respected in China as was evident by their being elected to the office of Vice-Chairmen of China's highest military organ, hesitated momentarily, then General Chen Haching, the most senior spoke up.

"Mr. Chairman. We were wondering when you believe it will be appropriate for us to take some more aggressive action the U.S.?"

"Interesting question, Gentlemen, and worth taking under advisement for possible presentation to the National People's Congress. What do you have in mind?"

"As the Americans are wont to say, 'all options are on the table'." The senior Vice-Chairman grinned slightly at his own joke. His demeanor belied his sense of humor. He was a tall man, with a receding hairline and an angular face with sharp rectangular edges that looked as if it had been squeezed and shaped within a powerful vise. He seldom smiled. He had entered the People's Liberation Army as an ordinary soldier and had overcome many obstacles to achieve his current position. He was a devout Communist.

"Ah, yes. All options. You mean war, of course – a direct war between the Chinese people and the United States. Is that not correct?" the Chairman responded.

"Yes, Sir. That is correct."

"It is as I had thought. I have previously informed The Standing Committee of the National People's Congress that I was expecting you to request this meeting and so I have prepared a few thoughts." The Chairman paused momentarily. "I wish to call your attention, once again, to the Selected Works of the revered Jiang Zemin, former Chinese President. You should note especially his theory of "Three Represents." Would one of you please explain this theory to me?"

"Certainly, Mr. Chairman," one offered. "First is to always represent the development requirements of China's advanced social productive forces. Second is to represent the progressive course of China's advanced culture. Third is to represent the fundamental interests of the overwhelming majority of the Chinese people."

"Good." "Where does war with America fit into the Three Represents?" the Chairman asked.

"Number Three?" volunteered one of the Vice-Chairmen.

"It is possible," replied the Chairman, "but let us look at that more closely. Who is the single largest purchaser of our goods and services?"

"America," they responded in unison.

"And does that not bring us great revenue to help our people better enjoy life?"

"Yes," They replied.

"And even in this economic crisis, does not America yet possess a formidable military power?"

Again, the three replied, "Yes."

186

"A wise man knows that it is foolish to back a wild animal into a corner, because if the animal has no way to go but through his pursuer, it becomes a dangerous situation. Is this not so?" The three nodded their agreement.

"And if the animal is wounded, is it not even *more* dangerous?" More nodding. "So, at the moment, trade with America is in our fundamental interest and to avoid unnecessary loss of comrades' lives is also in our fundamental interest."

"Mr. Chairman," the senior Vice-Chairman queried, "I thought that you looked forward to the day when China, not America, was the world's greatest super-power?"

The Chairman laughed. "You are perfectly correct. I am in favor of putting America under the Chinese thumb, but at the proper time, and that time is not now, but it is close. Let us discuss our position. Americans are destroying themselves from the inside out. If we are patient, in just a short time we will not have to fight them. We will merely have to bring forth a large wind and they will crumble inwardly from two forces of their own making: one, the corruption and incompetence of their own politicians; two, the greed and cowardice of their people. Americans do not have the patience to properly build for the future. Even before this disaster, they have been tearing themselves apart.

"First, consider how they came to glory in the world. It was through three things: their Constitution, their religious beliefs, and their national spirit. Today, their two major parties are so greedy and power hungry that they both try to re-interpret their Constitution for their own political gain, even when it is harmful to the country and the people, which is why the most important of the "Three Represents" for we Chinese leaders is the fundamental interest of the overwhelming majority of the Chinese people. American politicians today do not understand this concept of the interests of the overwhelming majority of the American people.

Their fundamental purpose is to further their own personal interests. Today, their religion is irrelevant. Finally, today they have lost their national spirit.

"There is an increasing gap between the very rich and everyone else. Today, they have mostly become a people more willing to beg for governmental handouts than to work for honest pay. They possess an entitlement mentality. They are beggars and if they do not get their handouts, they protest, but only because they know that their laws will protect them, no matter how vile their protests. They burn their own flag and get away with it because no one has the courage to stop them. If someone does stop them from desecrating their own flag, they sue for harassment against the one who is protecting their flag. They are a weak, sick people. Concurrently, their politicians are the most corrupt in the world. The greatest capability of their politicians is their ability to lie when covering up their corruption. Their major company executives are like their politicians. They are only interested in the money they can make by trading with us. They have no national concern or spirit. Why would we risk the lives of our soldiers fighting what is about to become a paper tiger?" The Chairman chuckled, and called for a bourbon and coke. He took a sip, then continued. "What particulars are working in our favor?"

The senior Vice-Chairman responded. "Our relations with both Africa and the Middle East have improved immensely. These governments are currently friendlier to us than to the arrogant Americans. I believe our access to oil is greater than America's and we have gained a near parity in technology with America. Our SIGINT (signal intelligence) is the most advanced and comprehensive in the Asia-Pacific region and our exploitation of the revolution in military affairs (RMA) is much further advanced than most of the "China Watchers" could imagine, especially the development of our "new concept" directed energy weapons—such as our high powered microwave and high powered lasers. We are capable of destroying America's satellite systems and establishing information dominance in the Pacific at any time we choose."

"You are correct," said the Chairman. "Our gain in technology comes from three areas: First, we are getting better in our own development of technology. Second, many of America's big businesses, as well as corrupt politicians are willing to sell anything, including their souls, if the money is right. Thus, when America has new technology, we know that we soon will have it."

"But what if they survive and do not crumble?" asked one of the three.

"Then we will play our strongest non-war card," advised the Chairman. We currently are the largest holder of America's debt. If we were to call it all as due and payable, we could bankrupt their entire economy. Also, we are working with several nations to remove the U.S. Dollar as the underlying world reserve currency. As the world reserve currency, they can print money to cover their debt. Once they are removed from this position, they will no longer be able to print more dollars; the world will no longer accept it. Their currency will be useless, causing great inflation and further destroying their economy. They will then have to produce goods and services which they are no longer capable of doing on the scale necessary to maintain. When that time comes, America will crumble economically.

"This is when we must be prepared to attack them militarily. As you know, we are working on the Golden Dragon project. We are only a few short years, maybe only months away from being able to launch the Dragon, but our current course is to continue helping them to self-destruct. As I said earlier, Americans do not have the patience for a protracted conflict; however, we Chinese have been living such protraction for generations. We are the Middle Kingdom. We were here before either the Christians or the Muslims and we shall be here when all of their nations are gone. We will continue to assist our Muslim comrades as they attack America and its interests, wherever and whenever. This is another major advantage we have. The radical Muslims hate the Americans even more than they love their own children. They willingly sacrifice their own children to kill Americans. This is very confusing to Americans. It frightens them and it does not cost us a thing. We shall continue to use the "Three Represents" as a theoretical guide for our current central leadership to draw up key policies and directives. Keep this in mind. I would also suggest that as the leaders of the Central Military Commission, we have a responsibility to apply the "Three Represents" in our development of the People's Liberation Army. We are not the only ones who can cause a war. If America decides upon a course of war, which is not likely, we must be ready to defeat them. You see, as long as the West, including America, delude themselves into believing that continued trade will make us become like them, we have an advantage. They are afraid to challenge us on their mistaken opinions so it leaves us free to pursue our own courses of action. When the time is right, we will swallow them."

"And Taiwan?"

The Chairman grinned wryly. "Yes. The intention is to bring Taiwan back as part of one China. Currently Taiwan and the United States have a treaty that would create a delicate international situation if we were to move against Taiwan at this time. However, that time is also near. Since the fall of the Soviet Union, it has been a unipolar world with America being the sole superpower. That will soon change and that will be the time to reunite Taiwan with the Chinese people. When we know that America no longer has either the willpower or the capability to stop us, we will move against Taiwan. America will not dare to oppose us and the world will know the Americans are a cowardly, beaten people. We will still adhere to former President Hu's "Four Nevers." We will 'never sway in adhering to the one-China principle, never give up efforts to seek peaceful reunification, never change the principle of placing hope on the Taiwan people, never compromise in opposing 'Taiwan Independence'."

The generals rose, bowed, and left the room.

The Chairman smiled and sipped on his drink. *China will be the acknowledged number one world power under my leadership as Chairman. I will be revered as the second Mao!*

ABOUT THE AUTHOR

Ernie Webb is U.S. Army retired. After military retirement, he spent fifteen years as a leadership and organizational improvement consultant with Fortune 500 companies around the world.

While serving in Vietnam, Ernie received the Purple Heart and five decorations for valor, including two Silver Stars.

Ernie and Pat, his wife of 48 years, raised two wonderful children, both now married: Mike and his wife Jane, Maureen and her husband, Mike Thorsen. Pat and Ernie have two wonderful grandchildren, Makenna and Miller.

God bless America!